Toying with fate

Or, Nick Carter's narrow shave

Nicholas Carter

Alpha Editions

This edition published in 2024

ISBN : 9789357962742

Design and Setting By
Alpha Editions
www.alphaedis.com
Email - info@alphaedis.com

As per information held with us this book is in Public Domain.
This book is a reproduction of an important historical work. Alpha Editions uses the best technology to reproduce historical work in the same manner it was first published to preserve its original nature. Any marks or number seen are left intentionally to preserve its true form.

Contents

CHAPTER I. THE MYSTERIOUS OLD MAN .... - 1 -
CHAPTER II. SEARCHING FOR CLEWS. .... - 6 -
CHAPTER III. THE IDENTIFICATION. .... - 14 -
CHAPTER IV. A PECULIAR INTERVIEW. .... - 22 -
CHAPTER V. AN IMPORTANT PACKAGE. .... - 31 -
CHAPTER VI. THE THREAT. .... - 38 -
CHAPTER VII. EAVESDROPPING. .... - 46 -
CHAPTER VIII. A WOMAN SCORNED. .... - 54 -
CHAPTER IX. MORE EVIDENCE. .... - 62 -
CHAPTER X. LENA'S STORY .... - 71 -
CHAPTER XI. ACTING A PART. .... - 81 -
CHAPTER XII. CAUGHT IN A TRAP. .... - 90 -
CHAPTER XIII. BLACKMAIL. .... - 98 -
CHAPTER XIV. TIGHTENING THE COILS. .... - 107 -
CHAPTER XV. MURDER IN HELL'S KITCHEN. .... - 118 -
CHAPTER XVI. THE MILLIONAIRE'S GUEST. .... - 124 -
CHAPTER XVII. BACK TO THE RED SPOT. .... - 130 -
CHAPTER XVIII. THE FATE OF A SPY. .... - 136 -
CHAPTER XIX. THE KNOCK-OUT DROPS. .... - 142 -
CHAPTER XX. AN INCORRUPTIBLE DETECTIVE. .... - 148 -
CHAPTER XXI. THE CARD CLEW. .... - 154 -
CHAPTER XXII. THE BIRD IN THE DEATH TRAP. .... - 159 -
CHAPTER XXIII. CARTER AND HIS QUARRY. .... - 164 -
CHAPTER XXIV. STARTLING DEVELOPMENTS. .... - 169 -
CHAPTER XXV. A TERRIBLE COMPACT. .... - 175 -
CHAPTER XXVI. THE DARK JAILERESS AGAIN .... - 181 -

CHAPTER XXVII. FOUND IN THE TIDE. - 187 -
CHAPTER XXVIII. A FAIR FOE. - 193 -
CHAPTER XXIX. THE BACK TRAIL. - 198 -
CHAPTER XXX. THE MASTER DETECTIVE'S LITTLE GAME. - 204 -
CHAPTER XXXI. IN MOTHER FLINTSTONE'S DEN AGAIN. - 210 -
CHAPTER XXXII. MULBERRY BILLY'S "FIND." - 216 -
CHAPTER XXXIII. THE COST OF A SECRET. - 222 -
CHAPTER XXXIV. BETWEEN THE WALLS OF DOOM. - 228 -
CHAPTER XXXV. A COMPLETE KNOCK-OUT. - 234 -
CHAPTER XXXVI. THE PARRICIDE. - 240 -
CHAPTER XXXVII. CARTER'S ESCAPE. - 246 -
CHAPTER XXXVIII. JUSTICE'S ROUND-UP. - 252 -

CHAPTER I.
THE MYSTERIOUS OLD MAN.

"Move on, old man, and go home!"

It was the stern voice of one of New York's finest policemen that uttered these words.

"Home! I wonder where it is?" muttered the old man to whom the policeman had spoken, and a shudder ran through his frame, as he slowly moved down the street.

As he reached the corner near old St. John's Church, on Varick Street, he paused, rubbed his eyes and gazed dreamily around him.

For some time before the policeman had addressed him he had been standing inside the church, looking through the railings into the churchyard.

His form was bent by decrepitude and sorrow, and his hair was as white as the flaky snow that clung to the steeple of the old church, the bells of which had just sounded the knell of the dying year.

The old man only halted on the corner for a minute, and then, crossing Beach Street, he shuffled along until he reached the center of the block, where he came to a standstill in front of an old-fashioned house, which was unoccupied.

Then, as if a faintness had come over him, he grasped the rusty iron railing to prevent himself falling to the ground, and he closed his eyes, as though the sight of the snow-covered houses was too much for him.

The policeman had followed him at a distance, and was watching him from where he was standing on the corner.

"Poor devil!" muttered the guardian of the peace, as he swung his nightstick back and forth. "I wonder who he is! He seems weak! Perhaps at one time he amounted to something. God save me from ever coming to his condition. I wonder why he stands so long in front of that old empty house, which has been closed for twenty years, to my knowledge! I'll watch him a while, but I won't molest him, poor devil!"

As the policeman concluded his soliloquy the old man straightened up and walked up to the door of the house, the old knocker on which he caught hold of and gave it a rap.

But suddenly, as if struck by some painful recollection, his hand fell to his side and he staggered back to the middle of the sidewalk.

"Strange," the policeman ejaculated, noting this action. "Perhaps he lived there at one time."

The old man looked up at the house, at which he gazed long and intently.

Then, suddenly arousing himself, he ambled back to the corner, stopping near the policeman. He looked confusedly around him, from the left to the right, and the policeman gazed at him closely, but spoke not a word. On his part, he did not seem to see the man in uniform. He stood bewildered, appearing not to know which way to turn.

"Why don't you go home, old man?" the policeman asked, this time in a softened tone of voice.

"Home!" the old fellow ejaculated—his voice was like a wail, a heartbroken sob. "Home! where is it?"

"The Lord bless you, man, how can I tell you, if you can't tell yourself?"

"Twenty years ago—twenty years behind darkened walls—and this——" He muttered the words in such a forlorn tone that the policeman stared at him.

"Your brain is turned, old gentleman."

The old man laughed and looked up into his questioner's face with a quizzical expression.

"My brain is clear, my friend," he replied, in a clear, harsh tone. "I have come from a prison—the world is strangely altered since I was in it before."

"In it before? Why, what do you mean? I suppose you will try and persuade me that you have been dead and have risen from the grave."

"Figuratively speaking, I have—I have been dead to the world—in prison at Sing Sing. Mark me well—Sing Sing Prison—for twenty years—to-day I was released. See me now. I am old, decrepit, hardly able to walk. Once I stood erect, my hair was as black as the raven's wing, and now—look at me, a wreck without home or friends. Wife, children, all gone! I have never seen nor heard of them since the day I was taken out of yonder house a prisoner, by the unjust, hard, and cruel decree of a so-called court of justice. Twenty years! A prisoner, buried alive, as it were."

"You had committed a crime?"

"No. I was innocent, but powerful conspirators plotted against me—the evidence was perjured—and I—I—was entombed."

"You say you lived in yonder house twenty years ago?"

"Yes, and no man carried his head higher than I did. I was rich—but bah! what is the use of rehearsing those things to a stranger! Hardened as you are by association with crime, you would not believe my story. You would think that I was romancing. Things have sadly changed in this neighborhood."

"You may bet they have."

"Once all these houses were occupied by rich people, but to-day they are the abodes of the poor and the outcast."

"What is your name?"

"My name! It matters not. Good night."

"Well, well, keep your secret, old man. God bless you, and may this new year bring you happiness."

"Happiness! I shall never know that again. Good night, again."

He moved off slowly, and the policeman watched him until he turned the corner into West Broadway, when he proceeded to patrol his beat.

As the policeman moved away, a dark form came out of a near-by doorway and hurried around the corner.

The man was tall, he wore a long ulster with the collar turned up around his neck, and a slouch hat was pulled down over his eyes. He followed closely in the old man's trail.

The old man halted several times, and as he did so his form seemed to lose its decrepitude. As the light from the street lamps shone upon his face it could be seen that his eyes glared like two living coals; he threw his hand aloft, and so fierce and startling was the action that the man who was following him halted and shrank back for an instant, as if he had been struck.

"Vengeance!" the old man hissed, and then he started on again.

The street was deserted, save by the old man and the man who was following him.

The former walked on, looking up at the tall warehouses and store buildings, muttering to himself.

More than once he put his hand up to his head and gazed about in a bewildered manner.

His limbs shook under him, for a long time had passed since they had been used to such exertion.

The fresh air came so strangely upon him that he panted for breath.

Suddenly he halted in front of an old-fashioned three-story brick building near Chambers Street. A beacon-shaped red lamp was burning over the doorway, and upon the front pane of glass was painted:

THE RED DRAGON INN.
Established by William Sill—1776.

It was an old landmark in the neighborhood, and it had always been a hostelry. In revolutionary times it was a post roadhouse, and was famous as the headquarters of many of the British officers. During later days it became the resort, at the noonday hour, of many of New York's most staid and solid merchants, whose places of business were in the vicinity.

At this time the ground floor was occupied by a man who ran a saloon and restaurant, and who rented out the upstairs rooms to transient lodgers. No improvements had been made about the place, and it stood just as it did when it was conducted by its original owner.

As the old man paused in front of the inn the sound of voices and the clinking of glasses came from within. He walked up to the door and opened it. Then he stepped into the saloon, staggered up to the bar and, in a low tone, ordered a glass of toddy, which was supplied to him.

A number of men were seated at the tables, drinking, and none of them paid any attention to the newcomer, who drank his toddy while standing and leaning against the bar.

The old man placed his empty glass back upon the counter, and facing the bartender, said:

"I want a room for the night."

"There is only one empty," the bartender replied. "It is in the attic."

"That will answer my purpose."

"It will cost you one dollar."

The old man drew a purse out of his pocket, took out the amount, and handed it to the bartender, who asked:

"Do you want to retire now?"

"I do," the old man answered.

"I will show you the way up."

"It won't be necessary. I am familiar with every room in the house. Many a time I have stopped here in other days. If you will tell me which room I am to occupy, I will go up to it."

"The second room in the back part of the attic on the left of the stairway is the one. You will find a lamp on a table in the hall on the second floor."

"All right."

The old man left the room, while the bartender gazed after him with curiosity. He climbed the stairway and reached the second floor, where he found the lamp, and then proceeded upstairs to the attic room.

An hour after he retired, the house was silent, all the midnight revelers having gone home, and the bartender having closed up the saloon.

New Year's Day dawned bright and clear.

The proprietor of the Red Dragon Inn opened the barroom, and at nine o'clock the bartender came downstairs.

For a time the two men stood talking.

There were no customers in the place.

At last the bartender asked the proprietor if he had seen anything of the strange old man who had come in after midnight.

The proprietor said that the old man had not appeared.

"Did he request you to call him?" he inquired.

"No," the bartender answered. "Shall I go up and ask him if he wants breakfast?"

"Yes."

The bartender ascended to the attic.

The door of the room which the old man had been assigned to stood ajar.

The man knocked, but there was no answer. He pounded again and shouted. Still no answer. Finally the man pushed the door open. A terrible sight met his gaze. Stretched out upon the bed he beheld the old man, with his throat cut from ear to ear. His hands were folded across his breast, and he was covered by the coverlet of the bed. Evidently there had been no struggle.

The bartender uttered a cry of alarm, but he did not enter the room.

As soon as he recovered from his surprise he dashed off downstairs, crying "Murder!" at the top of his voice.

Instantly the house was aroused, and in a short time a great crowd congregated in the street in front of the door.

CHAPTER II.
SEARCHING FOR CLEWS.

Early on New Year's morning Nicholas Carter, the famous detective, arrived in Jersey City on a train from Chicago, where he had been investigating a diamond case, which he had closed up successfully.

Danny, his chauffeur, met him at the station, with his powerful touring car; and in a few minutes they were crossing the Hudson River on the downtown ferry over to Chambers Street.

They had just landed and were beginning to get headway along that thoroughfare, when their attention was attracted by a loud commotion in the street.

Leaning over, Carter beheld the crowd congregating in front of the Red Dragon Inn, which was almost opposite. He heard the cries of murder.

Instantly the veteran's energies were aroused. He forgot all about his not having had breakfast, and springing out, he pushed his way through the crowd and entered the barroom of the Red Dragon Inn.

There he found the proprietor pacing up and down in a state of nervous excitement.

A policeman was also there, and to him Nick applied for information.

"I can't make head nor tail of it," the policeman replied to Carter's inquiry. "I've sent word to the police station, Mr. Carter, and I am expecting the captain every minute."

"Have you been upstairs?"

"No, sir. I thought it best to wait until the captain arrived."

"Where is the bartender?"

"Standing over there," and the policeman pointed to the man, who was leaning against the bar.

Carter stepped up to the bartender and asked:

"What is your name?"

"George Terry," the bartender answered.

"How long have you been employed here?"

"Three years."

"I believe you discovered the murder?"

"I did, sir."

"At what time?"

"About twenty minutes ago."

"Do you know the man?"

"No, sir, he is a stranger to me."

"What is his name?"

"I forgot to ask him."

"Don't you keep a register?"

"No, sir."

"What time did the man arrive?"

"Shortly after midnight."

"Did he have any luggage?"

"No, sir."

"Tell me all about your conversation with him."

"As I said, he came in here shortly after midnight. He seemed weak and exhausted as he slipped up to the bar. He requested me to make him a hot toddy, which I did.

"After he had finished his drink he asked me if I could let him have a room for the night, and I told him that the attic room was vacant and he could have that. He paid the price out of a well-filled purse.

"I offered to conduct him up to the room, Mr. Carter, but he said it would not be necessary, because he was familiar with the house, he having stopped here on various occasions twenty years ago. He left the room, and that was the last I saw of him until I discovered his murdered body, when I went up to the attic to call him and opened the door of the room he occupied."

"You heard him say he had stopped here on various occasions twenty years ago?"

"Yes, sir."

"What is the proprietor's name?"

"Henry Lancaster."

"How long has he conducted this place?"

"Ten years."

"Do you know the name of the man from whom he purchased it?"

"I do not."

"Has any one been upstairs to the murdered man's room since you made the discovery?"

"No one has been near it. Everything is undisturbed. I did not enter."

"I will speak to the proprietor."

Carter approached Mr. Lancaster, who was a middle-aged man of affable manners.

"The bartender informs me that you have conducted this place for about ten years," the detective said, as he came up to Mr. Lancaster.

"I have owned it for nearly eleven years," Mr. Lancaster replied.

"From whom did you purchase it?"

"A man named Peter Wright, who had been the proprietor for nearly a quarter of a century."

"Is Mr. Wright alive?"

"He is."

"Where does he reside?"

"At the Cosmopolitan Hotel, across the street. He is a bachelor, and entirely alone in the world, all of his relatives having died. He is an Englishman by birth, and a courtly old gentleman. He has a moderate income to live on, and he is enjoying himself in his declining years. All of the merchants of old New York knew him, and when he conducted the Red Dragon Inn it was famous as a chop house.

"Mr. Wright's acquaintance is extensive," added Lancaster. "If you see him, he may know something about the murdered man—if the man spoke the truth when he said that he used to stop here twenty years ago."

"I shall surely call upon Mr. Wright, and ask him to take a look at the remains."

At this moment Carter felt a heavy hand laid upon his shoulder. He turned around and beheld the captain of the precinct, who had just arrived.

"I am glad to see you, Mr. Carter," the officer exclaimed. "You can help us in this, and as usual I suppose you have gleaned considerable information?"

"I have found very little," the detective replied.

"Will you help us?"

"Certainly."

"My mind is relieved. I hope you'll take full charge of the case."

"What about headquarters?"

"I will take care of that. While you have charge, the people at headquarters will not interfere."

"Have you sent out an alarm?"

"Yes."

"Let us go up to the attic room. Request your men to keep every one downstairs."

"I will do that."

The police captain issued his instructions to his men, and then he and Carter proceeded upstairs to the attic room in which the body of the victim lay.

The captain stood out in the hall on the threshold, while the detective entered the room.

Carter stepped up to the side of the bed and scrutinized the face of the victim closely in silence.

"His throat was cut while he slept," Nick remarked, looking toward the captain.

"Do you see any sign of the weapon with which the crime was committed?" the police official asked.

"Not yet."

Carter turned around and commenced to inspect the room.

For nearly fifteen minutes he was engaged in the work, without uttering a word.

The police captain watched him with close attention.

The detective went over the ground with the avidity of a sleuthhound scenting for a trail.

Every nook and corner of the apartment was inspected, until the detective stood by the window, the sash of which was raised. He looked at the sill and then uttered an exclamation.

"What is it?" the police captain asked, entering the room and stepping up to Carter's side.

CHAPTER III.
THE IDENTIFICATION.

Carter conducted Peter Wright upstairs to the attic room in which the body of the victim lay.

The coroner was making an examination, but he stepped aside, so as to allow Mr. Wright to see the face of the murdered man.

The former proprietor of the Red Dragon Inn looked at the ghastly white countenance long and intently.

All of the persons in the room watched him in silence.

Several times the old man shook his head back and forth and his brow became contracted.

Finally he looked at Carter and shook his head dolefully.

"There is a certain familiar expression about that man's features," he said, in a tone of awe, "but for the life of me I cannot recall who he is. If he were a patron of the Red Dragon Inn while I was proprietor, he has changed so that I cannot remember him."

"I am very sorry that you are not able to identify the body, Mr. Wright," the detective said. "Will you kindly accompany me downstairs. I want to have a private talk with you."

"Lead on, and I will follow."

The detective led the way down to the parlor.

As soon as they were inside the room he closed the door. Presently he and Mr. Wright were ensconced in easy-chairs.

"Permit your memory to wander back ten or twelve years to the time when you owned this place, and see if you can recall the name of any one of your patrons who was sent to State's prison."

Mr. Wright started.

"By Jove!" he exclaimed.

Carter smiled and his eyes sparkled.

"What startles you?" the detective asked, with an assumed air of surprise.

"Nothing startles me," Mr. Wright rejoined.

"Then what is it?"

"That man is Alfred Lawrence—he has changed mightily—it is no wonder I did not recognize him. But I know him now."

"Who was Alfred Lawrence?"

"He was one of my old customers. He was sent to Sing Sing for fifteen years for forgery. Don't you remember the famous Lawrence will case?"

"I have a slight recollection of it. The trial took place while I was away in Europe, and I read very little about it."

"I will tell you about it."

"Do so."

"Alfred Lawrence was a well-to-do produce merchant, who had an office on West Street and lived on Beach Street.

"His uncle, after whom he was named, was the senior member of the firm. Old Alfred Lawrence was a bachelor.

"When he died a will was found, and in it he left all his estate to his nephew.

"Simeon Rich, another nephew, and his sister contested the will. They claimed that it was a forgery and that Alfred Lawrence had forged his uncle's signature.

"The case came up before the surrogate and the fight was a bitter one on both sides.

"Lawrence's wife, with whom he had lived unhappily, went before the referee and swore that she had seen her husband forge the will. Her testimony was corroborated by Blanchard, the chief witness, who was Lawrence's butler.

"It was hinted at, at the time, that Mrs. Lawrence and Simeon Rich were very intimate.

"The will was broken. Lawrence was arrested, tried, convicted, and sent to State's prison.

"Then people forgot all about him."

"What became of Mrs. Lawrence?" asked Carter.

"She lived for a time in the Beach Street house. A year after her husband's conviction the house was closed up and Mrs. Lawrence and her child disappeared. The house has remained closed ever since."

"Then there was a child?"

"Yes—a girl—she was about twelve years old at the time."

"What became of Simeon Rich?"

"I do not know."

"How was the estate divided?"

"That I do not remember."

"Lawrence, you say, was a customer of yours?"

"He was, and he was a mighty fine fellow. I always believed he was innocent, notwithstanding the fact that all the evidence was strong against him."

"And you believe that the murdered man is this same Alfred Lawrence?"

"I do."

"Is this all the information you can give me, Mr. Wright?"

"It is."

"What was the number of the old house on Beach Street in which Lawrence resided?"

"I don't remember, but you can find it easily. It is near Varick Street, and it is the only house on the block that is closed."

"Ah!"

"Some one is at the door," said Peter Wright.

Carter arose from his chair and opened the door.

The police captain entered the room, followed by a policeman.

"Mr. Carter," he said, "here is one of my men, Officer Pat Maguire; he saw the murdered man last night."

"Did he?" Carter queried, casting a searching glance at Maguire, who replied:

"That I did, sir."

"Sit down and tell me all about it."

Pat Maguire took a seat.

"This morning," he said, "I reported at the station house and I heard about the murder. The instant I heard a description of the man read I concluded it was the poor, forlorn, down-and-out old chap with whom I had talked last night while on my beat.

"I came around here, took a look at the body, and I saw that it was the old man. Then I instantly told the captain about the conversation I had with him, and he brought me here to see you."

"Tell me about that conversation, Maguire."

Policeman Maguire gave Carter a clear account of the conversation which he had held with the old man and described how he had acted.

When he concluded, Mr. Wright ejaculated:

"You see, Mr. Carter, that corroborates what I told you. There are no reasonable doubts now about the man being Alfred Lawrence."

"Why did he try to enter that house on Beach Street?"

"I cannot tell."

"There is a deep mystery here," remarked Carter, "one which I intend to solve. Gentlemen, I must leave you. Please keep silent about what you have told me."

Before any one could utter a word, he had slipped out of the room.

"A strange man," the police captain remarked, as soon as Carter was gone. "Why has he left the room without giving any intimation of what he was going to do?"

The information which had been imparted to Carter by Mr. Wright and the policeman was important. He was certain now that the murdered man was the ex-convict, Alfred Lawrence.

It was his intention to probe into that man's history and learn more of the details of the will case and the trial.

In doing this, would he be able to discover the motive of the murder?

After leaving the Red Dragon Inn the detective at once—without waiting to go home—went to a near-by telephone exchange and called up the keeper of Sing Sing Prison.

From this man he learned that Lawrence had been released early the day before, that he had been furnished with clothing and a small sum of money, and that he started for New York.

"What train did he leave on?" Carter asked of the keeper.

"The eleven-ten," the keeper replied.

"Was he an exemplary prisoner?"

"Yes."

"Did he have any visitors call on him?"

"None."

"Are you sure?"

Many would have looked upon such a task as Carter had set out to perform as hopeless.

The railroad detective who was stationed at the depot was unable to furnish Nick with any information.

Carter made inquiries of the porters and others, but none of them remembered seeing any man who answered to Lawrence's description.

Finally, he left the depot and went outside to the cab stand.

Here he commenced to question the drivers.

At last he found a man who, in reply to his question, said:

"I drove the old chap downtown in my cab."

"Do you think you would be able to identify him if you should see him again?" Carter asked.

"I do," the cabman answered.

"Will you come with me?"

"What for?"

"I want you to take a look at a man and see if he is the same person whom you drove downtown."

"I can't leave my cab."

"Drive me down to the Cosmopolitan Hotel."

"I'll do that."

Nick sent Danny home, got into the cab, and was driven away.

He had his reasons for not telling the cabman anything about the case.

Before he questioned him further he wanted to see if the murdered man was the same person whom the man had had for a fare the previous day.

The cab stopped in front of the Cosmopolitan Hotel and the detective alighted. He and the driver crossed the street and entered the Red Dragon Inn.

To the chamber of death the detective conducted his surprised companion.

When they entered the room Carter pointed to the corpse and asked:

"Is that the man?"

"Dead!" the cabman ejaculated, as he started back, after having glanced at the face of the murdered man. "Yes, sir, it is the man, all right. He has been murdered!"

"Yes."

"Did you fetch me down here to place me under arrest?"

"No."

"I know nothing about this."

"Come with me."

"I'll go with you, but I swear——"

"There, there, my man, don't get excited. You will not be arrested—rest easy on that score."

"But——"

"Wait until we get outside, and then I will tell you what I want you to do."

They returned to the cab and stood on the sidewalk near it.

Carter was silent for a short time.

Suddenly he looked up into the pale face of the cabman and asked:

"Where did you drive him?"

"You mean——" the man stammered. The question had been asked so suddenly that he was slightly confused.

"I mean the man whose body lies over there in the Red Dragon Inn."

"I drove him down to the Manhattan Safe Deposit Company. He got out of the cab, told me to wait for him, and then he went into the building, where he remained for nearly half an hour. When he came out he paid and dismissed me."

"When he paid you did he display any large amount of money?"

"He had quite a large-sized roll of bills in his hand."

"Did you drive away immediately after you received the money for your services?"

"I did."

"And you did not notice in which direction the old man went?"

"He went back into the building."

CHAPTER IV.
A PECULIAR INTERVIEW.

Carter lapsed into silence after the cabman had answered his last question.

It was clear to him now that Lawrence had secured money at the Manhattan Safe Deposit Company.

Did he get the money out of a box, which he owned, or from some one connected with the company?

The detective proposed to find out. He happened to be acquainted with the cashier of the safe deposit company, so he ordered the cabman to drive him to the gentleman's house.

Fortunately, Carter found the cashier at home, and he was received by him in his library.

"Were you acquainted with an Alfred Lawrence?" the detective inquired of the cashier as soon as he was seated.

The gentleman started in surprise, and asked:

"Why do you ask that question?"

"I want information," Carter replied, with a smile. He paused for a moment, and then he continued: "I can see from the manner in which you started that you knew Alfred Lawrence."

"Yes, I did know Alfred Lawrence, and I always regarded him as an honest man. In spite of the fact that he was tried and found guilty of forgery, I have always believed he was innocent. But why do you come here asking about Lawrence?"

"Lawrence was murdered at the Red Dragon Inn early this morning."

"No! It can't be true!"

The gentleman bounded out of his chair and, standing in the center of the room, gazed at Carter with an expression of astonishment upon his face.

"It is true, nevertheless," the detective replied.

"I saw him yesterday. He had just been released from Sing Sing Prison."

"Please be seated and try to be calm. I want you to recall to your mind all that occurred yesterday between you and Lawrence. It is important that you should remember everything."

"I will try and do as you request."

The gentleman resumed his seat, and for some time he bowed his head, resting it upon his hand.

The detective remained quiet.

Patiently he waited for the cashier of the safe deposit company to speak. He desired to let him have plenty of time in which to recall to his mind all that had happened between him and the murdered man on the previous day.

Finally the gentleman raised his head and gazed intently into Carter's face.

"This is a great shock to me," he remarked, as he passed his hand over his forehead. "Lawrence came into my office about two o'clock.

"At first I did not recognize him on account of the great change that had been wrought in him.

"When I learned who he was I was glad to see him.

"He sat down and told me about his prison experience.

"In years gone by we had been friends.

"When he was tried I did what I could to help him.

"The evidence was too strong against him, and he was convicted.

"When he was sent to prison he left in my care some securities to dispose of. I sold them and placed the money on deposit with the Bank of North America.

"I wrote to him about it, and he said that he desired me not to communicate with him again until he should be free. Then he would call upon me. If I were to die I was to provide in my will that the money should be placed with some trust company for him.

"Well, as I said, he called on me yesterday. He asked me for two hundred dollars, and I gave it to him."

The gentleman paused.

"How much was the full amount?" asked Nick, upon whom the cashier's information was making a clear impression of innocence on the part of Alfred Lawrence.

"About seven thousand dollars," the cashier answered.

"Did Lawrence talk about his family?"

"He did not."

"Did he talk about any one?"

"All he said was that he intended to prove that he was not a forger."

"Did he say how he was going to do it?"

"No."

"Were you ever acquainted with Simeon Rich?"

"No."

"Is he living in the city?"

"I don't know."

"And you don't know what became of Lawrence's wife and child?"

"I do not."

"Did you know that Lawrence's house on Beach Street has remained vacant for years?"

"No."

"When Lawrence left you did he say where he was going?"

"He did not."

"Did he say that he would call on you again?"

"He promised to call and see me to-morrow."

"Did Lawrence run a safe deposit box?"

"He did. He had one with our company."

"Did he open it yesterday?"

"No. He told me that he intended to open it to-morrow."

"Did he have the key?"

"He did."

"Do you know the number of the box?"

"I do not."

"To-morrow I will find out the number for you."

"Can't you do so to-day?"

"Why?"

"I want to examine the contents of that box."

"You will have to wait until to-morrow, Mr. Carter. Then I will get permission for you to open the box."

"I suppose I'll have to wait."

"I am sorry that I can't help you to-day."

"So am I."

Carter gave the cashier an account of the mysterious murder at the Red Dragon Inn and then he departed, promising to call on him at his office early the next morning.

So far he had progressed fairly well with the case, though he had not secured any information which would throw light on the mystery.

The murdered man's identity was established and Carter had learned something about his history.

But that was not much.

Who could have committed the crime?

Was Lawrence murdered by a common thief or by one who was afraid of him and desired to put him out of the way?

Carter asked himself these questions.

He was not prepared to answer either one of them.

He had discovered no clew.

He had learned nothing upon which he could base a theory.

Leaving the cashier's house, he dismissed the cabman, and, hailing a taxicab, rode home, where he went to his study and sat down to smoke and think.

It was now evening. He had not wasted a moment since early in the morning, but he was not satisfied with his work. He had looked through the directory and had not been able to find in it the name of the man who had been instrumental in sending Lawrence to State's prison.

Did he have any suspicion that that man could have anything to do with the murder?

If he did not, then why was he so anxious to find out what had become of that man? He wished he had a more accurate description of the man who had entered the barroom of the Red Dragon Inn after Lawrence.

"That man may know nothing," he muttered as he thought about him, "but, nevertheless, I should like to find him.

"Who is he?

"What was he doing in the inn?

"Did he simply step in to get a drink, or did he follow Lawrence in?

"I'm puzzled."

The detective arose from his chair and commenced to pace back and forth across the room.

All the time he puffed away vigorously on his cigar and blew the smoke out in a long stream. Whenever he was annoyed about anything he always smoked in this way. He was so deep in thought that he did not hear a knock on the door until the person without had knocked several times.

Carter halted in the center of the room and called out:

"Come in."

The door was opened by Nick's butler and Peter Wright entered the room.

At a glance the detective saw he was excited.

"I'm glad you are in, Mr. Carter," Wright ejaculated, as he sank down in a chair.

He was puffing and blowing from exertion, and it was several minutes before he became composed. He mopped his brow with a large red bandanna and laid his hat down on the floor by the side of his chair.

"It was a peculiar experience," he ejaculated, looking at the detective, "very peculiar—very peculiar——"

Mr. Wright had a rapid way of speaking when he was excited, and he had a habit of repeating certain words and phrases to emphasize what he said.

"It was deucedly peculiar," he repeated, after a slight pause.

Carter could not help smiling as he said:

"Mr. Wright, you forget that I know nothing about it."

"That's so—confound it! I am so excited I can hardly collect my thoughts. But it was a deucedly peculiar experience, all the same," he replied.

"Tell me all about it."

"Tell you all about it? So I will—yes—yes. Peculiar—it was very peculiar——"

"No doubt. Try and collect your thoughts."

"I will."

Mr. Wright mopped his brow for the twentieth time, blew his nose, and then, rolling his bandanna up into a ball, threw it into his hat, saying, as he rested his elbows upon the arms of the chair and leaned forward:

"Mr. Carter, I think I have important information for you."

"That is what I want," the detective replied.

Nick was perfectly calm.

Not a muscle of his face moved.

But those shrewd eyes of his sparkled like two gems.

"It was this way," Mr. Wright continued, after a momentary silence: "After you left me I returned to my room in the hotel and sat down to glance at the morning newspaper. I could not remain quiet for any length of time, because my mind was dwelling continuously on the murder.

"Well, an hour passed. I was pacing up and down the room trying to recall to my mind everything I had known and had heard about Lawrence, when there came a knock at my door.

"I called out for the party to come in, and a tall, handsome, stylishly dressed woman entered the room.

"I was taken by surprise and was slightly confused. I thought at first the woman had mistaken my room for some one else's. But she looked at me very calmly, and when I did not speak she said:

"'Are you not Mr. Wright?'

"Instantly I pulled myself together and acknowledged that I was the individual. I invited her to be seated.

"As far as I could remember, Mr. Carter, I had never seen the woman before in all my life.

"'You are Mr. Peter Wright?' she asked again, as soon as she was seated, and she placed considerable emphasis upon 'Peter,' looking me straight in the eyes with such intensity as if she were endeavoring to read my most secret thoughts.

"'My name is Peter Wright,' I said, and I commenced to experience a creeping sensation all over me.

"Never before had I been in such a position.

"It may have been my imagination, but I thought that she was making an effort to exert some influence over me.

"Well, that is neither here nor there. It is a waste of time for me to go into details about my feelings———"

"Go on," Carter interrupted, "tell your story your own way, and do not make any attempt to abridge it. I am deeply interested."

"Let me see—oh, yes. As I said, I thought she was trying to hypnotize me.

"As soon as I said that I was Peter Wright she asked:

"'Were you the owner of the Red Dragon Inn at one time?'

"I replied in the affirmative, and I saw a smile encircle her lips.

"'You don't remember me,' she said, after a pause.

"'Indeed, I do not,' I replied. 'I cannot recall that I ever saw you before.'

"'No doubt, no doubt,' she murmured. She glanced around the room and ran her hand across her forehead. 'I have changed wonderfully,' she went on. 'Twenty years works wonderful changes in all of us,' and she smiled, with the sweetest smile I ever beheld upon the face of a woman.

"'We all change,' I interpolated, and she replied:

"'You are right. I was a girl when you saw me last, and now I am a woman. Mr. Wright, do you not remember Isabella Porter?'

"The instant she mentioned the name I remembered her.

"Her parents used to live a few doors from the Red Dragon Inn. Her father was a produce merchant. When she was a small girl I used to give her pennies to spend. Her father died and her mother moved out of the neighborhood. I lost track of them, and I had not seen nor heard of Isabella until she appeared in my room.

"To tell you the truth, Mr. Carter, even after she had told me who she was, I studied her face, but could not see a line in it that was familiar to me. I believed she was Isabella Porter, all the same.

"I told her that I remembered her name, and then for a time she was silent. She bowed her head, and seemed lost in deep thought.

"Suddenly she glanced up at me.

"'I've called to see you on a peculiar errand,' she informed me.

"'What is it?' I asked.

"'One night about ten or eleven years ago,' she said, 'a man called on you at the Red Dragon Inn and gave you a package to keep.

"'The man was a stranger to you.

"'On the package was written the name of Edward Peters.'

"'You put the package in your safe and the man never called for it.'

"She paused and fastened her eyes upon me, Mr. Carter, with that strange, uncanny, searching look—it was certainly peculiar, *very* peculiar!

"I recalled the incident distinctly, but something within me seemed to tell me to pretend ignorance about the package, to try and draw her out and find out what she was aiming at, so I said:

"'I don't remember any such incident.'

"Isabella Porter started and her face darkened.

"'You don't?' she ejaculated, in a tone of annoyance.

"'No,' I replied. I was perfectly calm now, you see, and I had full command of my senses.

"Isabella eyed me closely, but I returned her gaze unflinchingly.

"Why I acted in this way I cannot tell. An unseen force seemed to be guiding me.

"'What did you do with the contents of your safe?' Isabella asked.

"'When I sold the place,' I replied, 'I removed the contents of the safe. I placed the paper in a box and locked it up in the safe deposit vault. Since that time I have never looked at it,' which was the truth.

"'Then the package must be in your box,' Isabella ejaculated, and her countenance brightened. 'Mr. Wright, I want that package.'

"'If it should be among my papers,' I replied, 'I can't see why I should deliver it to you. It does not belong to you.'

"She bit her lips with annoyance and exclaimed:

"'I must get possession of that package, Mr. Wright.'

"'Why?' I asked.

"'I can't tell you the reason why,' she answered. 'You would not understand if I were able to explain. But, Mr. Wright, please let me have that package.'

"'What is in it?' I asked.

"'I can't tell you,' she replied.

"'Oh, well,' I said, with a false laugh. 'It is nothing to me. To-morrow I will hunt through my papers at the safe deposit company and I will see if the package is among them.'

"'Can't you look to-day?' she asked, with great eagerness.

"'No,' I replied; 'to-day is a holiday and the vault is closed.'

"'Then I suppose I must wait. What time shall I call upon you to-morrow?'

"'About eleven o'clock,' I answered.

"'I will be here on time,' she said, and she arose from her chair.

"'Where are you living?' I inquired.

"'At No. — West Nineteenth Street,' she replied.

"'With your mother?'

"'My mother has been dead five years. I reside in a flat alone.'

"'Are you married?'

"'No, no,' she laughed.

"I wanted to question her further, but I refrained.

"Isabella departed.

"As soon as she was out of the room I locked the door.

"I had lied to her, Mr. Carter. The box with the contents of my old safe in it was not in the vault of the safe deposit company, but it was resting under my bed.

"I pulled it out into the center of the room and unlocked it. I examined the contents, and at last came across the package with the name of Edward Peters written across the face.

"It was sealed.

"I broke the seals and tore off the wrapper.

"Another wrapper was beneath, and upon it was writing.

"I read the indorsement.

"As the words appeared before my eyes I was so overcome with excitement that I could not move or think for some time."

Mr. Wright paused, looked at Carter, put his hand into the breast pocket of his coat, and pulled out a large package.

CHAPTER V.
AN IMPORTANT PACKAGE.

"This is the package," Mr. Wright ejaculated, as he held up the bundle. "I have not opened it."

"What is the indorsement?" Carter asked.

"Listen and I will read."

"Read."

"'Papers relating to the Lawrence will case.'"

"The deuce you say!"

"Read for yourself."

Mr. Wright handed the package to the detective.

Carter took hold of it and read the indorsement.

"The writing is bold and clear," he said. "No name signed to it."

"It is peculiar," Mr. Wright rejoined. "It seems strange that this should turn up just at this time, and it is remarkable that I should have been impelled to act as I did."

"Yes," Carter remarked, and he became thoughtful, while he held the package in his hand and gazed at it fixedly.

"What do you suppose those papers contain?"

"We will examine them."

"Why was Isabella Porter so anxious to get possession of them?"

"That we will have to find out."

"Who was Edward Peters?"

"I can't answer the question."

Carter laughed as he glanced at Mr. Wright, who joined him, remarking:

"If I were not so excited I would never have asked such a question, Mr. Carter."

"I am aware of that."

"Let us examine those papers. There may be something in them which will furnish you with a clew."

"Or they may deepen the mystery."

Carter broke the seals and tore off the wrapper.

Five documents fell into his lap.

Mr. Wright drew up his chair close to the detective's side.

Carter picked up one of the papers and read the indorsement:

"'Confession of George Blanchard, butler, employed by Alfred Lawrence, Esq.'"

"Phew!" Mr. Wright gave a prolonged whistle.

His and the detective's eyes met.

For some time they did not speak.

"Confession of George Blanchard," repeated Mr. Wright.

"We will read it," the detective remarked, and he opened the paper.

Mr. Wright leaned back in his chair.

Carter cleared his throat and commenced to read:

"'I, George Blanchard, knowing that I am about to die and to be called upon to face my Maker, desiring to make reparation for grievous wrongs and sins which I have committed, do make the following confession, hoping thereby to ease my conscience. May God have mercy upon my soul!

"'I was born in Manchester, England, and at the age of twenty I came to America.

"'Shortly after my arrival in New York I was engaged by Alfred Lawrence, Esq., to act as his butler, and I went to work at his house, No. — Beach Street.

"'Mr. Lawrence was engaged in business with his uncle, after whom he was named.

"'Old Mr. Lawrence died, and when the will was read it was found that his nephew was left all of the property.

"'Simeon Rich, another nephew of the deceased, proceeded to contest the will, and he claimed that Mr. Alfred Lawrence had forged the document.

"'Previous to the death of old Mr. Lawrence, Mr. Alfred Lawrence and his wife became estranged.

"'They used to quarrel frequently.

"'Mrs. Lawrence was a cold, willful, and heartless woman.

The detective took the Blanchard confession out of his pocket and showed the doctor the signature.

"This is my signature," the physician said, after he had glanced at it, and instantly he thawed out and became interested. "What is that paper?"

"A confession of a man named George Blanchard," the detective answered. "He was at one time a butler for a Mr. Alfred Lawrence."

"I remember the man. He died from injuries received in a runaway. I never knew what the confession related to.

"A man named Peters was with him all the afternoon before he died. I came up to the cot just as he signed the paper, and Peters requested me to witness the signature, which I did.

"My mind was busy with other matters, and I never thought to ask what was in the paper.

"I signed the death certificate, and, if my memory does not play me false, I think Peters claimed the body and buried it.

"A month later Peters was brought to the hospital in a dying condition. He had been stabbed, I think, in some dark street downtown.

"I recognized him as the man who had been with Blanchard and who had requested me to sign the paper.

"He died without recovering consciousness.

"I can't tell whether any one claimed his body or not."

"The records at Bellevue will show that?"

"Certainly."

"Doctor, we are greatly obliged to you for this information."

"Why are you so anxious———"

"I can't tell you anything just at present———"

"I understand, Mr. Carter. Well, if I can be of any further service to you, don't hesitate to call on me."

"Thank you."

Carter and Wright departed.

As soon as they were outside in the street, the latter turned to the former and said:

"What are you going to do next?"

"We will go over to Bellevue," the detective rejoined.

At the hospital Carter proceeded to examine the record of deaths.

After a long search, he found the name of Edward Peters.

"Here it is," he said, turning to Peter Wright and holding his finger on the name.

"Read what the record says," said Wright.

"'Peters, Edward. Forty, unmarried, native of England. Cause of death: stab wound in back, over left lobe of heart. Occupation: butler. Where employed: No. — Fifth Avenue. Name of employer: Mrs. Isabella Porter. Body claimed by Mrs. Porter. Date, September 21.'"

"Well!" Wright ejaculated, and he looked at Carter, with a quizzical expression upon his face.

"More mystery," the detective rejoined.

"Peters stopped at the Red Dragon Inn on the night of September 20."

"How do you know that?"

"I put the date on the wrapper of the package."

"Did you leave that wrapper in your room?"

"I did."

"From this record, it appears that the man was Mrs. Porter's butler."

"Yes. She never had a butler when they lived on West Broadway, and I was not aware that she had gone to reside on Fifth Avenue."

"Mrs. Porter's daughter was named after her?"

"Obviously!"

"Let us go to your hotel. When Miss Isabella Porter calls on you to-morrow, tell her that you could not find the package."

"I'd like to know how she learned about it."

"That we will find out all in good time."

"I will put these papers away in a safe place."

"Do so."

It was quite late when the detective and Wright reached the hotel.

Carter recovered the wrapper which had been outside of the package. He sealed the documents up in an envelope, and had the bundle locked up in the hotel safe.

When he reached his house, an hour later, he did not retire to rest.

As soon as he locked the door of his sanctum, he proceeded to change his clothing.

In a quarter of an hour he had changed his appearance so completely that his most intimate acquaintance could not have recognized him.

What did he intend to do?

From the manner in which he acted, it was quite clear that he did not propose to remain in. He examined his notebook before leaving the room, and as he went out he muttered:

"We will see what kind of place Miss Porter lives in."

CHAPTER VI.
THE THREAT.

Carter desired to learn something about Isabella Porter.

Her appearance at this time and her anxiety to secure the papers which had been left in Mr. Wright's possession so many years before seemed peculiar.

As the detective reviewed the incidents, and recalled the record of Peters' death to his mind, he was almost certain that the man had been attacked by some one who desired to put him out of the way.

Was Peters' death planned because he had in his possession these damaging papers?

Carter pondered over this question.

The circumstance was puzzling.

Why was no attempt ever made until now to get possession of the documents?

How did Isabella Porter come to know or suppose that they were in the possession of Mr. Wright?

Was it any wonder that Carter was in a quandary when these questions were presented to his mind?

He did not know what to think.

He was in the dark.

There was a veil before his eyes, figuratively speaking.

He felt that Isabella Porter had some connection with the mystery of the Red Dragon Inn, but what this connection was he could not determine.

Presently he arrived at the address on West Nineteenth Street.

It was an apartment house. He went into the vestibule and examined the names on the letter boxes.

The name of the woman was not among them.

"It is as I supposed," the detective muttered, "she does not live here, and she gave Mr. Wright this address simply as a blind."

To make sure that he was not wrong in his surmise, Carter called on the janitor and questioned him.

The man did not know any woman by the name of Isabella Porter, and he was sure that no woman answering to her description lived in the house.

"She had some deep object in view when she gave that false address," the detective thought. "The discovery alone is sufficient to make one suspect her."

Early the next morning the detective called at the address on Fifth Avenue which he had found in the record of Peters' death.

No one knew anything about any person by the name of Porter.

He returned to the hotel, and went to Mr. Wright's room, intending to remain there until the woman called.

He sent a message to the cashier of the safe deposit company, stating that he had important business on hand, and he would see him later in the day.

Noon arrived, and Isabella Porter did not appear.

Carter was impatient.

"I've wasted the whole morning," he remarked to Wright.

"That woman promised to call early," Wright rejoined. "Do you think her suspicions were aroused?"

"That I cannot tell."

"It is curious."

"Very."

Carter strode over to the window and looked out into the street. He was in a brown study.

What should he do?

Just then some one knocked on the door, and the detective opened it.

A messenger boy stood before him.

"I've got a note for Mr. Peter Wright," the boy said.

Mr. Wright took the note, and opened it. He glanced at it, and then turning to the boy, asked:

"From whom did you receive this?"

"A man," the boy replied.

"Where was he when he gave it to you?"

"In the barroom of the Humberland House."

"What kind of a looking man was he?"

"He was tall, had a smooth face and black hair."

"What did he say when he gave you the note?"

"He said simply to fetch it down to you."

"Was that all?"

"That was all."

"Did he pay you?"

"Yes, sir."

"You may go."

"Wait, sonny."

It was Carter who spoke. He had remained quiet during the time Peter Wright was questioning the lad.

"Let me see that note?" he asked, and Wright handed the message to him. He read it, and a smile crossed his face.

Then he looked at the boy, and asked:

"Did you ever see the man before?"

"No, sir," the boy answered.

"You may go."

When the messenger was out of the room, Carter turned to Mr. Wright, and said:

"This note shows that the woman suspected a trap."

"No doubt," Mr. Wright rejoined. "Read the note to me. I just glanced at it."

"'*Mr. Peter Wright.*

"'DEAR SIR: I cannot call on you to-day. I thought you were a gentleman, but I have discovered that I cannot trust you. After I left you yesterday I learned that you held a conference with Nicholas Carter, the detective, and he commenced to make inquiries about me. That man had better beware of how he meddles with my affairs. I know that you have that package in your possession, and if you turn it over to that detective, you will live to regret it. Yours very respectfully,

"'ISABELLA PORTER.'"

"Humph!" Mr. Wright ejaculated, when the detective finished reading. "*That* for her threat!" and the old man snapped his fingers together, while defiance shone in his eyes.

"One thing is certain," Carter remarked.

"What is that?"

"We're watched."

"By whom?"

"Probably by the man who gave the note to the messenger boy."

"What are you going to do?"

"I am going to call on the cashier of the safe deposit company."

Half an hour later the detective was in the office of the safe deposit company. He and the cashier visited the vault, and, after some hesitation, the latter opened Lawrence's box.

It was empty.

When this discovery was made, Carter uttered an exclamation of chagrin.

"Who could have removed the contents?" the cashier ejaculated. "Lawrence told me positively that he had valuable papers in this box."

"They have been removed, but whether recently; or years ago, we cannot tell," the detective said.

"It is annoying."

Carter left the vault and started uptown.

So far, he considered that he had made very little progress with the investigation.

He reached the Humberland House, and entered the café.

It was four o'clock in the afternoon, and quite a number of men were in the place. He thought that there might be a chance of learning something here, and that was the reason why he had stopped.

The man who had given Isabella Porter's note to the messenger he thought might come into the place. He sat down at one of the tables, and proceeded to inspect the men around him.

His attention was attracted toward a tall man who was seated at the next table, with a short, stout man.

The man was well dressed.

There was something about his manner the detective did not like, and he looked at him more closely than he otherwise would have done.

All of a sudden it came to him that this man answered the description of the man who had given the messenger boy Isabella Porter's note.

Carter acted cautiously, so that the man would not notice that he was watching him.

They spoke in low tones, and it was some time before the detective was able to catch a word they said.

He leaned back in his chair and listened.

The men were drinking.

After a time they commenced to talk louder, and the detective was able to hear.

A man of less experience would have started, and perhaps betrayed himself when he heard the stout man address his companion as Rich.

Not so Carter. He did not move in his chair, or show any sign that he had heard a word.

His eyes were fixed on a painting on the opposite wall, and apparently he was examining it.

"Well, Rich," the detective heard the stout man ejaculate, "I think you made a mistake."

For a while this was all he heard, for the man spoke in low tones again.

But this was sufficient to make Carter more deeply interested in those two men.

"Can this be Simeon Rich who conspired against Lawrence?" he asked himself.

There was a chance that the man was in no way related to the murdered man.

After a time the detective heard the man Rich remark:

"Isabella made a mistake."

"I don't know about that," the stout man rejoined, and at the same time he lighted a fresh cigar, while he leaned back in his chair and blew the smoke up in the air over his head.

"Darwin," replied Rich, in a low, clear, deep voice, "I think you are unnecessarily alarmed."

"I am not. I have heard a great deal of that man's ability."

"All such men are overestimated. When they are brought face to face with shrewd men they fail."

"Make no mistake. That man has circumvented shrewder men than we."

"Bosh!"

"Even at this moment he may be in possession of important evidence."

"How could he secure it?"

"I do not know, and yet I do not feel safe."

"I tell you, we have nothing to fear."

"You should never have had that letter of Isabella's delivered."

"The old fool will never dare to show it."

"That man has already been to Bellevue and examined the records."

"How do you know that?"

"I made inquiries."

"When?"

"This afternoon."

"Humph!"

"It was well I had him watched."

"In one way it was."

"Yes, in many ways."

The men rested back in their chairs, and were silent.

Carter had heard every word, and he was sure that the two men had referred to him, although they had not mentioned any names.

His heart beat violently, in spite of his stoicism.

Outwardly he was composed, but inwardly he was excited.

"Am I on the right trail at last?" he asked himself.

"Have these men had anything to do with the mysterious murder at the Red Dragon Inn? Ought I to suspect them?"

Darwin arose from the table, paid the cashier for what they had had, and then the two men strolled out of the café into the corridor of the hotel, when they halted near the newspaper stand.

Carter followed them openly but unobtrusively, and stood within a few feet of them.

The lobby was crowded with people, and it was easy to keep them under surveillance without the fear of attracting their attention.

"Well, Rich, what are you going to do?" Carter heard Darwin ask, after they had stood silent for some time near the door.

"I am going uptown," Rich replied evasively.

"To see Isabella?"

"Yes."

"Try and induce her to take a trip to Philadelphia, and remain there until things quiet down."

"She won't listen to that."

"Confound these women, anyway! If you had let me manage that affair, and kept her out of it, there would have been nothing to worry about. As it is, you went ahead without asking my advice, and the result may be that you have furnished that man with a clew which will lead up to our downfall."

"Always croaking, Dick!"

"No, I am not."

"What are *you* going to do?"

"I am going to take a trip down to Lem Samson's joint, and see if Brockey Gann has any report to make."

"What time to-morrow will you meet me?"

"Eleven o'clock."

"Where?"

"Here," said Darwin.

"If anything of importance has occurred, I will send you word."

"Then, good night."

They had walked out into the street, and now they separated, one starting uptown and the other walking down to the corner of Twenty-fourth Street, where he halted to wait for a car.

For a moment or so Carter was in doubt about which one he ought to follow.

Richard Darwin had mentioned that he was going downtown to a place kept by a man named Lem Samson.

The detective was familiar with the place, which was one of the worst crooks' resorts on Houston Street, near Macdougal Street.

He also knew that Brockey Gann was the leader of a gang of thugs.

He had arrested Brockey several times, and once he succeeded in sending him to State's prison for a short term.

Carter saw Darwin start out toward the center of the street as a downtown car came along.

In an instant his mind was made up.

He ran out into the street and jumped aboard the car ahead of Darwin.

On the way downtown the detective made a close study of the man. He did not remember that he had ever seen him before.

Darwin had the appearance of a man in prosperous circumstances.

That he had been in the habit of associating with sporting men was quite evident from certain phrases which Carter had heard him utter.

At Houston Street Darwin jumped off the car.

CHAPTER VII.
EAVESDROPPING.

Carter did not act hastily. He waited until Darwin had turned the corner before he alighted from the car. Then he started after his quarry, whom he soon caught sight of hurrying along on the south side of Houston Street.

The detective kept on the north side of the street.

As he walked along, he made a few changes in his disguise, so that if he and Darwin were brought face to face again the man would not recognize him as the same person who had stood on the platform of the car with him.

Darwin entered the crooks' resort.

Carter followed him inside.

A number of men were leaning up against the bar.

Lem Samson, a tall, burly, broad-shouldered, red-faced man, with an ugly scar over his left temple, was serving out the drinks.

Darwin stepped up to the bar and spoke to Samson.

Carter got near them, and heard what was said.

"Have you seen Brockey?" Darwin asked.

"He hasn't been in this evening," Samson replied. "Did you expect to meet him to-night?"

"I did."

"Go into the back room and wait."

"Is any one in there?"

"No."

Carter sat down in a chair near the door of that room, and feigned intoxication.

No one paid any attention to him.

The minutes passed.

Then the door of the room opened, and a man entered. He was dressed in black. His coat was tightly buttoned up, so as nearly to hide the white handkerchief that encompassed his scrawny throat. His hair—and it was not very luxuriant—was of a foxy color, and combed straight down, giving the observer the idea that it had been operated on by the prison barber. Pitted pockmarks covered his colorless, lean face.

At a glance the detective recognized Brockey Gann.

The rascal cast his restless eyes around the room, as if he were in fear of some danger, and, thus shuffling up to the bar, he asked of Samson, in a hoarse tone of voice:

"Have you seen him?"

"He's waiting inside," Samson replied, pointing toward the back room with his thumb.

Brockey, as he passed Carter, looked at him.

The detective's head was bending forward, and, apparently, he was asleep.

"Jaggy," Brockey muttered as he passed into the room.

"I'm glad you have come at last, Brockey," the detective heard Darwin exclaim. "Sit down. Help yourself to the rosy."

"Thank you," Brockey replied, and he seated himself at the table, pouring out a glassful of liquor and swallowing it at a gulp.

Darwin handed him a cigar, which he lighted and proceeded to smoke.

"That's the stuff!" he ejaculated.

"What did you discover this afternoon?" Darwin asked, after a pause.

"Nothing much."

"Tell me what you did learn."

"Well, the cove left the hotel and went downtown to the Manhattan Safe Deposit Company.

"Then he returned to the house.

"I laid around the place for several hours, thinking he would come out. He did not put in an appearance, and I proceeded to make inquiries.

"Then I discovered that he was not in his room, and I knew he had left the hotel.

"I haven't been able to get on his trail."

"The deuce!"

"That cove is like an eel."

For a time the men were silent.

Carter realized that Brockey had been tracking him, and saw that in the future he would have to be more cautious.

It was only by a mere stroke of good luck that he had slipped out of the hotel unrecognized.

Finally, Darwin looked across the table at his companion, and said:

"I think I can trust you, Brockey."

"Think you can!" Brockey ejaculated. "You have done so, and never found me unworthy of the trust. You remember——"

The blood left Darwin's face when thus addressed, for a moment, and a paleness usurped its place.

"Why, Mr. Darwin, I was in hopes——"

"I think you are misunderstanding me. I know you—I can trust you, and it is not everybody I would; let that suffice. I shall want you to do something more for me."

"What is that?"

"Carter must be put out of the way."

"I begin to comprehend. That man has been the bitterest enemy that I ever had."

"You don't love him?"

"No."

"Then you will undertake the job?"

"For a consideration—yes."

"Oh, I don't expect you to do it for nothing. I will pay you liberally. But, remember, there must be no failure."

"I'll do my best."

"Your best!"

"That's what I said," retorted Brockey.

"You must not fail."

"There is a chance that I may."

"You must not."

"See here, Darwin, that cove is one of the worst terrors in the business."

"I am aware of that——"

"Well—it——"

"Well——"

The men were sitting with their elbows leaning upon the table, and they stared into each other's eyes for some time in silence.

"Say, Darwin," Brockey finally blurted out, "I don't like to be spoken to in that way. You talk as if you had a hold on me."

"I *have* a hold on you!" Darwin fairly hissed, and his face darkened, while his eyes shone like two coals of fire.

"So you think. But I have also a hold on you, my bully boy, and don't you forget it!"

Again a silence fell on them.

Darwin scowled.

Brockey smiled, showing a hideous gold tooth.

"We won't quarrel," Darwin at last remarked.

"I guess not," Brockey replied, with a chuckle.

"Will you do the work?"

"I told you I would."

"Then start out to-night to run him down."

"The exchequer is very low."

"How much will you need?"

"Five hundred down and five thousand when the cove is out of the way."

"That is too much."

"Don't talk in that way. You know it is not too much. You and that other chap are going to pull out a big stake."

"I am no fool, Darwin."

"One word from me, and———"

"Hush! We are in a public barroom, and you ought to be more cautious."

"Are you going to come to time?"

"I'll give you three hundred to-night, and to-morrow we will talk about the balance."

"Fork out the three hundred."

Darwin took a roll of bills out of his pocket, counted out the amount, and passed it over to Brockey, who smiled again and shoved the money into his trousers pocket.

"How will you proceed?" Darwin asked.

"I'll make up my mind later," Brockey replied.

"To-morrow I shall expect to hear——"

"Don't count on hearing to-morrow."

"Why not?"

"I may not be able to find him to-night."

"All right."

"I'll meet you here to-morrow afternoon at four o'clock. Are you going?"

"Yes."

"I guess I'll go with you."

Darwin and Brockey left the room.

They passed the detective, and Darwin said:

"Did you notice that fellow?" pointing to Carter.

"Certainly," Brockey answered. "He's got a jag on."

They halted in the center of the room, and looked back at the detective, who did not stir.

"Suppose he should be shamming?" Darwin remarked, in an undertone.

"G'way," Brockey retorted.

"He may have heard what we were talking about."

"Not much."

"I have a sort of feeling that he is a spy."

Brockey gazed intently at Carter.

Without uttering a word, he strode across the room and clutched hold of the detective by the shoulder, shaking him vigorously.

"Wosh de ma-asher!" Carter growled, making no attempt to resist. "Wosh de ma-asher," he mumbled, a second time, in a maudlin tone. "Lesh a fel' alone."

"Get up out of here!" Brockey exclaimed, and he jerked the detective out of the chair.

Carter struggled from side to side, and his acting was perfect.

No one in the place paid any attention to him and Brockey except Darwin.

"Shay, ain't chue a-goin' t' lea' up?" Carter mumbled, and he caught hold of Brockey by the arms, to steady himself.

"Where do you live?" Brockey asked.

"Nowhere."

The rascal was entirely deceived. He firmly believed that the detective was nothing more than a drunken "bum." He let go his hold on him, and, with a grunt of well-feigned disgust, Carter staggered out of the den.

Brockey and Darwin followed.

The detective disappeared around the corner.

The instant he was out of sight he straightened up and darted into the doorway of a house, where he made a change in his disguise. He was anxious not to lose sight of Darwin, and he hastened back around into Houston Street again.

He almost ran into Brockey, who had separated from Darwin, who was hurrying off up the street in the direction of Broadway.

Brockey did not recognize the detective, and, with an oath, he passed around the corner.

Carter started after Darwin. He reached Broadway a few seconds later than he, and by a lucky chance he was able to get on the same car with him.

Carter was sure that he had struck the right trail. Indeed, he was firmly convinced now that Darwin and Rich were implicated in the murder, that they had formed together some dastardly plot.

The detective did not make any effort to surmise what that plot was.

It was too early yet to start to theorize.

By the detective's side on the platform of the car Darwin stood, entirely unconscious that the man whom he had paid Brockey to kill was near him.

When the car reached Thirty-first Street, Darwin jumped off, lighted a cigar, and strolled leisurely down the block, turning into Sixth Avenue.

Carter was not far behind him.

"I'm going to find out more about you, my lad," the detective thought, as he followed Darwin into a crowded dance hall.

It was nearly midnight, and the place was filled with men and women. A band was playing a popular waltz, and the floor was crowded with dancers. Loud laughter and shouts of maudlin mirth were heard on all sides.

Darwin halted near the entrance, and cast his eyes over the dancers.

"He's looking for some one," Carter mentally commented, as he noted his every action.

Darwin, at that moment, started up the stairway leading to the gallery.

The detective followed close behind him.

In the gallery, ranged along the railing, were small tables, at which merry parties of men about town and tenderloiners were seated, drinking.

The women were flashily and expensively dressed, and many of them were adorned with valuable jewelry.

Darwin, as soon as he reached the gallery, looked searchingly around.

Suddenly he started across the rear, and reached a table at the opposite side of which a young woman was sitting alone. The woman looked at him, and nodded coldly as he drew up a chair beside her.

Carter had also crossed the gallery, and he stood within a few feet of the table.

"What is the matter with you, Dora?" asked Richard Darwin, as he sat down and ordered a waiter to fetch a bottle of champagne.

"You know well enough what is the matter," Dora snappishly replied. "What's the use of you trying to feign ignorance?"

"You look real sweet when you talk in that way."

"How dare you!"

Dora's fine eyes flashed. She turned around in her chair, faced Darwin, and glared at him.

One could see that she was not in an amiable mood. She was angry about something. Her face was flushed, and she raised her hand, as if she would have liked to have struck her companion in the face.

"Here's the wine," Darwin exclaimed, with a forced laugh, as the waiter placed the bottle and glasses on the table. "Drink some, and see if it won't put you in a good humor."

"I want none of your wine," Dora retorted. "Keep it for your———"

"Yes, you do."

"I won't touch it. You and I are quits from this night forth."

"Phew!"

"Probably you think I don't mean it?"

"You *don't* mean it, my dear girl. Drink your wine."

"I want no wine that you have paid for. I want nothing from a man who will deceive me."

"I haven't deceived you, Dora. Indeed, I haven't. I don't understand what you mean."

"You scoundrel!"

The conversation was carried on in low tones, but it was exciting and intense.

Dora leaned back in her chair, as she called Darwin a scoundrel, and she looked him squarely in the eyes.

Carter, who had heard all that was said, was deeply interested.

CHAPTER VIII.
A WOMAN SCORNED.

Dora kept her eyes fastened on Darwin.

There was a peculiar glitter in them.

At first Darwin returned her gaze without flinching, but soon he commenced to move about uneasily.

For some time neither spoke.

A cynical smile played around the corners of Dora's lips.

"You are contemptible," she sneered. "Really, I should feel sorry for you if I did not despise you so intensely!"

"Really, Dora, I don't understand you," Darwin replied.

"You don't understand me? How can you sit there and say that? Where were you to-day at eleven o'clock?"

"Why—I—I——"

"Don't lie to me. Where were you?"

"I was in O'Rourke's restaurant."

"With whom?"

"Sally Rich."

"What were you doing in her company?"

"I met her by chance."

"You had an appointment with her."

"I did not."

"I was in O'Rourke's at the time, and I saw both of you."

"Spying on me?"

Darwin's face darkened, and he bit the ends of his mustache.

"I was *not* spying on you," Dora ejaculated. "I wouldn't spy on any one. But I am glad I've discovered your duplicity."

"You are jealous of Sally Rich," Darwin retorted.

"I am *not*! But I do hate her."

"I am aware of that. She hates *you*."

"She is a low——"

"Hush!"

"I will not hush! This is the third time that I have caught you with her."

"You don't understand. I have business with her brother——"

"Do you expect me to believe that? Not much! I'm not green. As long as you prefer that woman's society to mine, you may go with her, and I never want you to speak to me again."

"But, Dora——"

"Dick Darwin, my mind is made up."

"Do listen to reason, Dora."

"Good night."

Dora arose from the table, cast a contemptuous glance at Darwin, and walked into a side room.

"Confound that woman!" Darwin muttered, as he gazed after her. "If she turns against me, she may ruin me. I wish I hadn't met Sally Rich—at least, not for the present."

Carter heard what Darwin muttered, and he saw that the man was greatly disturbed.

"He's afraid of Dora, for some reason," the detective cogitated. "If I could get her out of here, unseen by Darwin, while she is in her present mood, I might be able to worm some information out of her. Shall I make the attempt?"

Carter looked into the next room, where he saw Dora putting on her cloak. He glanced at Darwin, who was leaning back in his chair in a brown study.

"Shall I try?" the detective thought, and he gazed after Dora, who was starting for the stairway. He saw that Darwin did not move, and he was still thinking.

In an instant his mind was made up, and he started after Dora.

She went out into the street.

Then the detective spoke to her.

"You are a stranger to me," she said coldly, with an air of affronted dignity.

"I am not such a stranger as you think, Miss Ferris. We have met several times," Carter rejoined.

"I don't seem to remember you."

"Perhaps not, in this rig. Will you come up to Sherton's with me and have some supper? I want to talk with you."

"Who are you?"

"My name is Nicholas Carter."

"Why, I——"

"You need not be afraid."

"I am not afraid."

"Will you accompany me?"

"I don't understand."

"I will explain when we get to Sherton's. There we can secure a secluded table, and no one will see us."

"It isn't that——"

"You will not regret it."

"I will go with you."

The detective and Dora had little to say until after the repast at Sherton's was placed upon the table, and they were alone.

"Now we can talk," the detective said, as soon as the waiter had left the room.

"You said you desired to secure some information from me?" Dora remarked.

"I do."

"I can't imagine what it is about."

"You have been friendly with a man named Dick Darwin?"

Dora started. She laid down her knife and fork, and looked at the detective, with amazement depicted upon every line of her handsome face.

"You heard what passed between us a while ago?" she ejaculated.

"I did," Carter calmly replied, and he smiled.

"Then you know that I have thrown him over?"

"Yes."

"I do not intend to have anything more to do with him."

"Do you really mean that?"

"I do. I am serious. I have made many sacrifices for that man, and he has treated me brutally."

"To-morrow you will change your mind."

"Mr. Carter, my mind is made up. Nothing will make me change it. I possess my father's nature. You were a friend of his, and you know how bitter he could be against any one for whom he formed a dislike. It is the same way with me."

"Then you will not hesitate to tell me all you know about Darwin?"

"Has he committed a crime?" asked Dora.

"Do *you* think he has?"

"I do not know."

"Neither do I," asserted Carter, with a smile.

"Then why are you so anxious to get information about him?"

"I can't tell you."

"Oh!"

Dora gazed at the detective. She picked up the glass of wine and commenced to sip the amber-colored liquid.

Carter was silent, but he watched her closely.

"Mr. Carter," Dora said, as she set down the glass, "I will tell you everything I know about that man."

"I thank you," the detective rejoined.

"I hate him."

Her eyes flashed. The hot blood mantled her brow, and she hissed out the words between her clenched teeth.

Now the detective saw that she was in earnest. He knew that she did hate Dick Darwin, and no power could make her become friendly with him again.

"How long have you been acquainted with him?" Carter asked, after a short silence.

"About three years," Dora answered.

"Where did you first meet him?"

"In London."

"What were you doing over there?"

"I was in the chorus of 'A Girl from New York.' We were playing over there at the Gayety."

"Were you introduced to him?"

"I was."

"By whom?"

"One of the other chorus girls, Sally Rich."

"Then you were acquainted with Miss Rich?"

"Yes."

"And her brother?"

"I know him."

"Well?"

"Yes."

"How long have you known him?"

"Four years."

"Where did you first meet him?"

"At Koster & Bial's, where his sister and I were singing together."

"Tell me all you know about Darwin."

"Give me time to collect my thoughts."

"Take all the time you desire."

Carter was succeeding better than he had calculated.

At first he did not suspect that Dora felt so bitterly about the manner in which she had been treated by Darwin. He congratulated himself on the move he had made.

As he watched Dora, and noted the fleeting shadows crossing her face, he was able to read almost all her thoughts. He saw that she had no compunctions of conscience, no tenderness for Darwin, and that she would tell all she knew about the man.

Did she know anything about the mysterious murder at the Red Dragon Inn?

The detective was unable to surmise.

Finally, Dora raised her eyes, and, gazing straight at Carter, she said:

"Dick Darwin is a cousin of Simeon Rich. His mother was a sister of Rich's father. He was educated in England, and he resided there until he was thirty years of age, when he came to New York to live.

"When his father died he inherited a small fortune. He soon ran through it. Then he became connected with several dramatic enterprises, and made money.

"Six months ago he took a company out on the road, and he became stranded in Cincinnati.

"I sent him money to return to New York.

"When he got here he was broke.

"For some time he and Rich did not speak, but after he got back to the city they patched up their differences and became as thick as two peas in a pod. Recently he got to going around with Sally Rich, unknown to me, and when I found it out, and chided him for it, he insulted me.

"Lately I have noticed that he was quite flush of money. He would not let me know where he got it from. When I would ask him what he was doing he would fly into a towering rage.

"To-day when I saw him with Sally Rich I made up my mind to sever our relationship."

Dora stopped talking and drank some wine.

"You have not told me *all* you know about Darwin," Carter remarked.

"How do you know that I have not?"

"I can tell from the manner in which you spoke that you have kept something back."

"What do you think I have kept back?"

"Was Darwin ever guilty of any crime?"

"Why?"

"I want to know."

"In England he was arrested for forgery."

"Ah!"

"He was released on bail, and he fled to this country."

"What did he forge?"

"Checks."

"Then he was never tried?"

"No. The charges are still pending against him."

"Is Dick Darwin his right name?"

"Yes."

"Were you ever present when he and Rich were together?"

"No."

"Don't you know what business they are engaged in?"

"I do not. I wish I did know."

"Did you ever hear Sally or her brother speak of a man named Lawrence?"

"Sally Rich once told me that she had an uncle by that name."

"Did she ever speak about him?"

"She only said that he died and left her and her brother a lot of money. They had to fight for it in the courts."

"Was that all she told you?"

"Yes."

Carter thought for some time before he asked another question. He reviewed all that Dora had told him. He had gained some important information, but not as much as he had expected. However, he was firmly convinced that Dora had told him the truth, and that she had concealed nothing.

"Miss Ferris," he said, after a time, "where was Dick Darwin on New Year's Eve?"

"I don't know where he was. He was with Rich. That I do know."

"How do you know?"

"I saw them together, going down Sixth Avenue, about nine o'clock at night. They did not see me."

"What time did you next see him?"

"At two o'clock in the morning."

"Where?"

"He came to my flat. He was greatly excited about something, and it seemed to me that he was very nervous."

"Didn't he say where he had been?"

"No."

"Did you ask him?"

"I did."

"And he would not tell you?"

"He would not."

"You say he was very nervous?"

"Very. His clothing was spattered with mud, and it seemed to me as if he had been in some kind of a rumpus."

"Was he intoxicated?"

"No."

"Is the clothing which he had on that night at your flat?"

"It is in his room there. But, Mr. Carter, for what purpose are you asking all these questions? What do you suspect?"

"I can't tell you now."

"You can trust me. I hate Dick Darwin so that I would help you to send him to prison."

"Would you do that?"

"I swear I would do it!"

"I am afraid——"

"Afraid I wouldn't?"

"Yes."

"Try me—trust me."

Carter looked at the woman intently for some time in silence.

Over and over again he asked himself whether he dare to trust her or not, and, at the same time, he was evolving a plan in his mind.

CHAPTER IX.
MORE EVIDENCE.

Dora was the first to speak and break the silence.

"Mr. Carter," she said, "I can see that Rich and Darwin are implicated in some affair which you are investigating. It may be a crime. It was committed on New Year's Eve, or you would not be so particular about that date. I feel sure of that."

"You are a shrewd woman," the detective remarked, with a smile.

"I am not very shrewd, but I can read character, and I am able to form conclusions by putting two and two together.

"You asked about Dick Darwin's clothing. If you desire to examine it, I will take you to my flat, and you can inspect it."

"Darwin may be there now."

"No, he is not. He can't get in. I have the key."

"I will go with you to your flat."

"Tell me first what case you are working on."

"That must remain a secret for the present."

"Ha, ha! I know!"

"You know?"

"Yes."

"What case am I working on?"

"The mystery of the Red Dragon Inn."

Dora laughed heartily.

Carter uttered an exclamation of annoyance.

"When you mentioned the name of Lawrence, I remembered that a man by that name had been murdered on New Year's Eve at the Red Dragon Inn, and I also remembered that it was stated that you were working on the case. You see, I know."

"Humph!"

"Now that I come to think of it, I remember reading that that man had just been released from State's prison. It was also stated that he was the forger of the Lawrence will. If that be so, then he was a cousin of Simeon and Sally Rich. Mr. Carter!"

"What is the matter?"

"A thought just occurred to me, and it startled me."

"What was it?"

"Do you believe that Simeon Rich and Richard Darwin had a hand in that murder?"

"I can't tell."

"Perhaps Rich was afraid of Lawrence——"

"We will not talk any more about this matter. We will start for your flat."

"I will help you."

"I believe you."

They arose from the table.

Carter put on his facial disguise, and then they left the restaurant.

Dora's flat was situated on Thirty-ninth Street, next to a theater. It was elaborately furnished in a style that evinced more money than good taste, and Nick almost shuddered at the array of showy furniture, useless bric-a-brac, draperies, and ornaments which crowded the little parlor into which she ushered him.

"Mr. Carter, I suppose you do not want to lose any time," she said, "so, if you will follow me, I will conduct you to Darwin's room."

Carter followed Dora along a private hall.

At last she opened a door, and led him into one of the bedrooms, remarking:

"This is the room."

After she had turned on the electric light, she looked around, and then she uttered an exclamation of surprise.

The room was in confusion.

Carter looked at Dora.

"He has been here and carted off all his things!" Dora ejaculated, as soon as she recovered the use of her voice.

"I thought you said he had no key?" Carter remarked.

"He has none. He must have come here before the servant left."

"What time does she leave?"

"Seven o'clock."

"Where does she live?"

"On Twenty-seventh Street."

While Carter was asking these questions, his eyes were wandering about the room.

On the floor, in a corner, he spied several pieces of paper.

He picked them up and smoothed them out.

Two were blanks.

The third had writing on it.

The detective read it.

His countenance brightened.

Dora noticed the change.

"What is it?" she asked.

"A note," replied the detective.

"From whom?"

"Rich."

"To Darwin?"

"Yes."

"When was it written?"

"On the afternoon of the day before New Year's."

"Is it important?"

"It may be."

"Will you read it?"

Nick examined her face intently.

"Do you still doubt me?" Dora asked.

"No," replied Carter, after a pause.

Nick was satisfied.

"You can rely on me to help you, Mr. Carter."

"I know it now."

"Will you read that note?"

"Yes."

"Do so."

"'December 31.

"'DEAR DICK: I was at the Grand Central this afternoon when he arrived. Followed him downtown in a cab. He went to the safe deposit company's office. Have placed a party on his trail. Meet me at seven o'clock to-night at the Knickerbocker Cottage. We will dine together. Yours in haste,

"'SIMEON.'"

"Then Darwin was with Rich that night?"

"No doubt."

Carter folded the paper and placed it carefully away in his pocketbook. He looked upon this note as an important piece of evidence. The "he" mentioned in it, he felt confident, referred to the man who had been murdered at the Red Dragon Inn.

According to this note, Rich and Darwin had dined together at the Knickerbocker Cottage.

It would be an easy matter to find out what time they left that place.

Another thing was clear, and that was that Darwin had taken fright about something, or he never would have removed his things from the flat in such haste.

Was this move an indication of guilt?

Carter turned to Dora, and asked:

"Do you know where Rich and his sister reside?"

"I do not," Dora replied.

"Did you ever hear Darwin speak of a woman named Isabella Porter?"

"I know that woman."

"Where does she live?"

"I do not know."

"Did you know that Darwin and Rich were acquainted with her?"

"Rich has known her ever since she was a small girl."

"What about Darwin?"

"He has only been acquainted with her a short time."

"When did you first meet her?"

"She was in Rich's company one night, and he introduced her to me."

"What do you know about her?"

"She is the daughter of a rich merchant, I believe. Her mother and father are dead. She has an income."

"Is that all you know?"

"It is."

It was too late to continue the inquiries further that night, he concluded, and he determined to go home, as long as he was uptown.

Carter was in a very thoughtful mood.

Many curious events had happened during the past twenty-four hours.

He was walking along leisurely, with his head bowed, thinking of plans for that day, and where he would go to make inquiries, when his attention was attracted to two men, who were walking ahead of him.

Instantly he raised his head and slackened his pace.

One of the men he recognized as Darwin.

The man's companion he had never seen before.

He could not get near enough to the men to hear their conversation.

At the corner of Fifty-second Street, the men separated, and Darwin started in an easterly direction.

Carter decided to follow him, and he gave up the idea of going home.

Darwin reached the east side of town, and turned into Second Avenue.

"What business has he over here?" the detective asked himself, as he kept on the trail of his quarry.

Between Forty-first and Fortieth Streets Darwin halted under a street lamp.

From his pocket he took a slip of paper, consulted it, and then went along examining the numbers of the houses.

Carter stopped in the doorway of the corner store and watched him.

At the same time he changed his disguise. He now looked as tough as any of the night prowlers in the questionable neighborhood.

Darwin entered a tall tenement.

Carter hurried out of his place of concealment.

He also went into the house and stood in the lower hall.

On each floor lights were burning.

As he looked up, he saw Darwin distinctly on the next floor, and he heard him knock on the door of the back room.

Darwin knocked a number of times, and no one opened the door.

When he started to descend the stairs, Carter walked out, and took up a position in a doorway of a house near the corner.

Darwin came out of the tenement, walked to the corner, and halted.

Back and forth he moved, and kept looking at the house.

The detective saw that he was uneasy. He wondered whom Darwin had come to see.

Darwin, after a time, came back to the tenement, and entered again.

Carter did not move from his hiding place.

His quarry only remained inside a minute or so, and then came out, going back to the corner and halting.

Carter came out of the doorway. He strolled up to the corner, and stopped within a few feet of Darwin, who saw and eyed him.

Two or three times the man made a movement as if he were going to address Carter.

But he hesitated.

The detective made no attempt to speak. He looked up and down the street, and appeared unconcerned.

Carter wanted to see if Darwin would speak to him. He judged that if he waited long enough the man would do so.

Darwin crossed the street, halted a moment, and then came back. He glanced sharply, suspiciously, at Carter.

"Excuse me," he said, as he came to a standstill, "do you live around here?"

"Are you addressing me?" the detective asked, in a disguised tone of voice.

"I am."

"Oh, well, yes, I live in that house down there," said Nick, pointing to the tall tenement which Darwin had twice entered.

"You do? What floor do you live on?"

"The top. Why?"

"I want some information about one of the tenants."

"Eh!"

Carter bent forward and looked at Darwin.

His acting was magnificent.

"Say, are you a fly cop?" he asked, with suspicion.

"No," Darwin replied quickly, "I'm not a detective."

"You haven't got the cut of one."

"No."

"What do you want to know?"

"Are you acquainted with a woman named Lena Peters?"

"You mean the woman who lives in the back room on the second floor?"

"Yes, yes."

"I know her by sight."

"Have you seen her to-night?"

"No."

"I've been to her room and knocked, but no one seems to be in."

"Did you have an appointment with her?"

"Not exactly an appointment."

"Oh!"

For a time they were silent.

Then Carter said, in an offhand way:

"What does Miss Peters do?"

"She sings in a concert hall over on the West Side," Darwin replied.

"I often wondered what she worked at to keep her out so late at night."

"Will you see her when she comes in?"

"I don't know."

"Are you going to remain here long?"

"All night."

"What for?"

"I watch stores on the block."

"Oh!"

"Why did you ask that question?"

"Will you deliver a message to Lena Peters when she comes home?"

"Certainly."

"Tell her that a gentleman named Richard called to see her, and that he wants her to come to his room the first thing after noon."

"Where are your rooms?"

"She is familiar with the address."

"Then she has called on you before?"

"Yes."

"At your rooms?"

"Yes."

"Have you ever been down here before?"

"No."

"I'll be sure and see Miss Peters."

"Here's a dollar for your trouble."

"Thanks."

Carter pocketed the money.

"I can depend on you?" Darwin asked uneasily.

"You can," the detective replied, and he hardly was able to repress a smile.

"Good night."

Darwin hurried away.

Carter did not budge from the corner.

That he had formed some new plan in his mind was evident, or he would have made a move to keep on the trail of his quarry.

"He said the woman's name was Peters—Lena Peters," the detective muttered, a few minutes after Darwin had disappeared around the corner.

"She has seen him a number of times. Can she be any relation to the man who died in Bellevue Hospital? If she is——"

Carter stopped musing, as he saw a woman, who had hurried around the corner, enter the tenement.

Instantly he started toward the house, and went in.

The woman was halfway up the stairs.

CHAPTER X.
LENA'S STORY.

Carter had entered the lower hall of the house without making any noise.

The woman's attention was not attracted toward him, so he stood back in the shadow and watched her.

She reached the landing, and, stopping in front of the door of the back room, she inserted a key in the lock, opened the door and went in.

Nick knocked on the door of the room.

The woman opened the door.

"What do you want?" she demanded, in surprise.

"Is your name Lena Peters?" the detective asked.

"It is."

"I want to talk with you."

Carter pushed his way into the room without ceremony, and closed the door.

The woman's face became flushed with anger. She stepped back from the detective, and her eyes flashed.

"What do you want?" she demanded, with a string of oaths, and she pulled out of her pocket a small pistol.

"Don't get excited," Carter quietly said, with a scornful smile. "Put up your pistol, Lena. I'm not going to harm you."

"Who are you?"

"I will tell you in a few moments."

"You are a stranger to me."

"I guess not."

As Carter said this, he pulled off his disguise.

Lena uttered a scream, and sank down into a chair.

"Nick Carter!" she gasped, and the pistol fell from her grasp into her lap.

"You recognize me now?" the detective said, with a smile, as he sat down.

From this it will be seen that he and the woman had met before.

After a pause, Carter remarked:

"Let me see, Lena, it is several years since we have had the pleasure of meeting. You haven't changed any since I last saw you."

"No," Lena stammered.

"At that time you were singing at the Empire, on the Bowery, if my memory does not play me false."

"Yes."

"A Western divine was robbed in the place of a large sum of money, and you were charged with the theft. It was a cowardly charge. I investigated the case——"

"And you found out that I was innocent."

"Right."

"Only for you, I might have been sent to prison."

"Correct."

"I——"

"Lena?"

Carter paused, and looked straight into the woman's eyes.

"What is it?" she asked.

"I want you to give me some information."

"Mr. Carter, I have always declared that if I could ever do you a favor for what you did for me I would do it."

"Now is your chance."

"What do you want to know?"

"Are you acquainted with a man named Dick Darwin?"

"Yes—why——"

"You have called on him a number of times?"

"Yes."

"Where?"

"He has a room in the Studio Building, at the corner of Twenty-sixth Street and Broadway."

"How long have you known him?"

"Only a few weeks."

"How did you become acquainted with him?"

"I——"

Lena hesitated. She looked at the detective, and her face turned pale.

Carter kept his eyes riveted upon her.

"Lena," he said, "you must not try to conceal anything from me."

"Mr. Carter, did Darwin employ you?" Lena asked.

"No. Why?"

"I just wanted to know."

"What if he had employed me?"

"I am unable to say."

Lena moved about uneasily in her chair.

Carter kept still.

He was giving the woman plenty of time to think.

There was no need to hurry, for he was confident that he would get out of her all the information he desired.

"Mr. Carter, what do you know about Dick Darwin?" Lena finally blurted out.

"Very little," the detective replied. "I want to learn what you know about him."

"You are as sphinxlike as ever."

"I have to be."

Another silence followed.

Lena arose from her chair and walked back and forth across the room several times. She resumed her seat again.

"I will tell you everything!" she exclaimed.

"That is right," the detective said, in an encouraging tone.

Lena leaned back in her chair, and for some moments she sat with head bowed.

At length she looked up at the detective, and said:

"I had a brother, whose name was Edward Peters.

"He was employed by a Mrs. Porter, who lived on Fifth Avenue.

"About ten years ago he was stabbed in the back, and he died in Bellevue Hospital.

"I always believed that some one murdered him, although I could never secure any evidence to prove it.

"He had for a chum a man named George Blanchard.

"Blanchard also died in the hospital.

"Previous to his death he made some kind of a confession to my brother in regard to a will case.

"I tried to get out of my brother what the confession was about, but he would not tell me.

"Three months ago I was looking through a trunk which contained some things belonging to my brother, and I found an old memorandum book.

"I opened it, and I was surprised to find written in it a short account of Blanchard's confession.

"I was interested.

"At the end of the confession I found a note."

"What was it?"

"I will get the book and read it to you."

"Do so."

Lena got up, walked over to a bureau, opened a drawer, took out a small, leather-bound book, returned to her seat, opened the book and commenced to read:

"'This night I stopped at the Red Dragon Inn. I gave the confession of Blanchard to the proprietor to lock up in his safe. I have seen Simeon Rich three times. I have told him that unless he pays me ten thousand dollars I will take Blanchard's confession to the district attorney. I did not let him know where I had put the documents. No one knows about the contents of the papers except myself. Doctor Thompson did not ask to read the confession when he signed his name as a witness.

"'Rich has promised to raise the money in a few days.'"

"Is that all?" Carter asked, when Lena stopped reading.

"It is."

"Let me have that book."

"Here it is."

The detective glanced at some of the pages, and then placed the book in his pocket.

"What did you do after reading that memorandum?" he asked.

"I knew Simeon Rich," Lena replied. "I met him some years ago. As soon as I read that memorandum I made up my mind that Rich would have to pay me well to keep silent.

"The thought came to me that perhaps he might have had a hand in my brother's death.

"I knew that Rich was quite sweet on Isabella Porter, the daughter of the woman for whom my brother had worked."

"She is dead now—I mean Mrs. Porter."

"Did you see Rich?"

"Yes; I hunted him up."

"Where was he living?"

"In the Studio Building, with Darwin, to whom he introduced me."

"How did you find that out?"

"I called on Miss Porter, whom I knew was living at the Gerlach."

"What did you say to Rich?"

"I told him that I knew about the confession, and I knew where it was."

"Was he frightened?"

"Yes. He held a conference with Darwin, and he then told me that they would let me know how much they would pay me.

"I demanded ten thousand dollars.

"We have had several conversations about the matter, and a few days ago I called on Darwin, and he gave me five thousand dollars on account.

"I then gave him a copy of the memorandum in regard to the papers having been left with the proprietor of the Red Dragon Inn."

"Have you seen him since then?"

"Once."

"Did he pay you any more money?"

"No, but he promised to do so."

From what Lena said, Carter knew now how it was that Rich had learned of the existence of the Blanchard confession.

The case was becoming clearer to the detective.

But, still, for all that, he had not secured any positive evidence to prove that Rich had anything to do with the murder.

"Lena," he said, "you say that you believe your brother was murdered?"

"I do," the woman replied.

"Do you think Rich had anything to do with it?"

"I am not sure."

"Will you be guided by me?"

"I will."

"I want you to put on your things and accompany me."

"Are you going to place me under arrest?"

"No."

"Then, what?"

"I am going to take you to my house. I want you to remain there until I have finished the case upon which I am at work."

"What is that?"

"The mystery of the Red Dragon Inn."

"And you suspect Rich?"

"I do."

"I have been reading about that case."

"You have?"

"Yes, and it has seemed strange to me that the detectives have not been able to find a clew."

"Will you accompany me?"

"Yes."

"I may need your assistance."

"I will help you, Mr. Carter, gladly."

"Let us start."

Lena put on her hat and coat, packed a few articles in a valise, and then she and the detective left the tenement.

Day was dawning when Carter reached his home. He conducted Lena to Mrs. Peters, his housekeeper, who gave her a room, in which she promised to remain.

Nick gave her a few instructions, and then he retired to his own room, where he threw himself down upon a couch and went to sleep.

It was late in the morning when Carter awoke. He had an interview with Lena, and then, after partaking of a light breakfast, he went downtown. Chickering Carter and Patsy Garvan, his two chief assistants, were engaged upon another case—in which, by the way, Nick was fated to play a prominent part—so he did not see them that morning.

Nick stepped into the Cosmopolitan Hotel, and saw Mr. Wright, who informed him that his room had been entered during the night by some one.

"I think I know who it was," the detective remarked, and then he departed, feeling sure that the person who had entered the room was Brockey Gann.

It tickled him to think that the rascal had been disappointed.

Carter called at police headquarters, and there he learned that other detectives had not made a discovery. He informed the chief inspector that he was following a promising clew, and that he might be able to render a report in a few days.

After leaving headquarters, he went uptown to the Knickerbocker Cottage. There he questioned the waiters, and at last he found the man who had served Rich and Darwin on New Year's Eve.

"Did you hear any of their conversation?" the detective asked the waiter.

"Only a little," the man answered. "They talked about some man who had just arrived in the city."

"Was any name mentioned?"

"Yes."

"Can you recall it?"

"I think it was Lawrence."

"What did they say about him?"

"I don't know."

"What time did they leave here?"

"About half past ten o'clock."

"Did you hear them mention where they were going?"

"A messenger boy brought Rich a note. He read it, and then I heard him remark that they had better hurry down to McKeever's saloon."

"Was that all?"

"Yes."

"Did you notice the number of the messenger?"

"It was seven-twenty-one."

"Do you know the boy?"

"He is attached to the office on Broadway and Thirtieth Street."

The waiter was unable to give the detective any more information.

Carter hurried to the office of the district messenger company.

There he found the messenger boy.

"Do you remember delivering a note on New Year's Eve to a man who was dining at the Knickerbocker Cottage?" the detective asked the messenger.

"Was he a tall man?" the boy queried.

"Yes."

"He was with a short, stout man?"

"Yes."

"I gave him the note."

"From whom did you receive it?"

"A man."

"Did you ever see him before?"

"No."

"Can you describe him?"

"He was pock-marked."

"Was he a tough?"

"Yes."

"Would you be able to recognize him again?"

"Yes."

Carter gave the boy a bill and told him not to mention their conversation to a soul.

From the boy's description he recognized Brockey Gann.

At McKeever's saloon the detective was fortunate enough to find the bartender who had been on duty on New Year's Eve. He was acquainted with the man, and as soon as he made himself known to him he readily answered all his questions.

They retired into a back room together, and as soon as they were seated Carter asked:

"Are you acquainted with a man named Simeon Rich?"

"I know who he is," the bartender replied.

"Do you remember if he was in here on New Year's Eve?"

"He was here with two men."

"At what time?"

"It was about eleven o'clock."

"Do you know the men who were with him?"

"One of the men was Brockey Gann—the other man I do not know, although I have seen him several times."

"How long did they remain here?"

"Only a few minutes. They held a whispered conversation and then went out."

"Did you hear anything they said?"

"Not a word."

This information only established one fact, and that was that Rich, Darwin, and Brockey were together on New Year's Eve.

Carter left the saloon.

He stood on the corner some time trying to determine what he ought to do next. He was almost positive that Brockey Gann was the scoundrel who had tracked the murdered man.

But how was he going to prove that?

This was a conundrum.

After a time Carter crossed the street and entered the establishment of a costumer.

CHAPTER XI.
ACTING A PART.

Carter secured a disguise from the costumer.

When he came out he looked like a typical tough.

Nick had some plan in his mind. He was sure that he was on the right trail, and that, such being the case, it would not be long before he would have forged every link in the chain of evidence.

While he was confident of success, still he did not know for a certainty who had committed the dastardly crime at the Red Dragon Inn, or what the real motive was.

He had suspicions, and he had collected strong circumstantial evidence.

But he wanted something more than this, and he was prepared to take any risk to obtain it. On his way downtown he stopped at a telephone station and called up Patsy, whose whereabouts he knew.

"Meet me downtown at my den within two hours," he said.

At last he reached Lem Samson's saloon, and entered.

A bartender was on duty.

Samson was not in the place.

Only a few hangers-on were lolling about.

Carter staggered up to the bar, and, calling for a drink, he cast his eyes about the room.

No one seemed to be paying any particular attention to him.

Nearly all of the men had records, and were known to the police.

The detective poured the liquor into a cuspidor when the bartender's back was turned. It was vile stuff, and he would not have drunk it unless he had been forced to do so by dire expediency.

After placing the glass back on the bar he walked into the back room and sat down. He picked up a copy of a sporting weekly and pretended to be deeply interested in examining the text and pictures.

But while he seemed to be reading, his eyes were wandering about the room, and every person who entered the barroom he scrutinized closely.

He was waiting for some one.

Was that some one Brockey?

Half an hour passed.

Carter had not stirred out of his chair.

The side door opened.

A man entered.

The man was Brockey Gann.

The detective saw him.

Still he did not move.

No change took place in his countenance.

Not a muscle moved.

Brockey looked around the back room.

His eyes fell on Carter, whose eyes were bent on the paper.

Brockey started, bent forward, and a change took place in the expression of his evil face. He uttered an ugly oath and stepped up to Carter, exclaiming:

"Why, Mugsey Donovan, when did you get out?"

Carter looked up, smiled inanely—a weak, silly, maudlin grin!—and replied:

"How are you, Brockey? Wot's dot youse said? Sit down an' have a ball wid me?"

"I asked you when you got out?"

"Six weeks ago. Wot cher goin' ter have? Name yer pisen?"

"I'll take some of the rosy."

"I've been on de tramp. I just dropped in here tinkin' I'd run up agin' youse."

"Oh!"

The bartender brought the liquor, and the two men were silent.

It will be well to explain that Mugsey Donovan was an old pal of Brockey's, whom Carter had arrested and sent to prison for highway robbery.

The rascal was still in Sing Sing.

It will be seen that the detective's disguise must have been perfect to have deceived Brockey as it did.

The scoundrel actually believed that he was talking to his old pal.

"How is it you got out so soon?" Brockey asked, after he had swallowed his liquor.

"Dey reduced me sentence," the detective rejoined.

"How was that?"

"I saved one o' de keepers' life."

"Go way!"

"I ain't jollyin' you."

"How did you do it?"

"An insane mug tried to escape from his cell. De keeper catched him an' den he made an attempt to kill de keeper. I seed it an' knocked ter mug out, see? Den de jailer petitioned de guvnor ter lea' me out."

"What are you going to do?"

"Dat's what I wanted to see youse about."

"I'm not into anything."

"Youse are not?" asked Nick dubiously.

"What do you mean by looking at me in that way?"

"Brockey, dis isn't a safe place ter talk."

"What do you mean?"

"Lea' go some place where we kin talk wid safety."

"I don't understand you."

"Brockey, don' youse try ter gi' an' old pal like me any sich a bluff as dat!"

"Mugsey——"

"Brockey, I'm on to yer game."

"You are on to my game?"

"Sure."

"Come——"

"Le's go some place where we kin talk wid safety." Brockey looked intently at the detective.

"I can't see what's in your nut," he ejaculated.

"Do youse want to talk over private matters here?" Carter asked, and Brockey drawled:

"No-o."

"Den le's go down ter some quiet joint."

"I'll be hanged!"

"Brockey, I knows wot game youse is working?"

"I am working no game. I'm on my uppers."

"Don't try ter gi' me eny game like dat, now, 'cause I'm on to de hull layout."

"You——"

"Wait."

"I——"

"Brockey Gann, I tort youse's never'd go back on an old pal in dis way."

"I'm not going back on you, Mugsey."

"Youse is when youse refuse to let me in on de game, so dat I kin git some o' de graft."

"You talk in riddles."

"I seed one t'ing."

"What's that?"

"I've got to speak more plain."

"You will."

"Den here goes—don't youse blame me if eny one hears it an' youse git into a trap. Las' winter youse was paid to——"

"Wait, Mugsey."

Brockey bent forward.

A strange expression was in his eyes.

"I'm waitin', Brockey," Carter said, and he returned the rascal's searching gaze.

"Where were you last night?" Brockey asked.

Carter laughed.

"Youse is comin' to yer milk now, Brockey," he remarked.

"Were you in this place last night?"

"Wot's de use o' talking here? It ain't safe, Brockey. Le' me gi' you a tip. Nick Carter may turn up here eny moment, an' youse an' me might not be able to git on to him, see?"

Brockey uttered an oath. His face turned pale. He glanced over his shoulder and his eyes wandered about the room.

"Ain't my advice sensible?" the detective asked.

"I guess it is," Brockey replied.

"Den le's git out o' here."

"All right. But I'll be hanged if I can understand what——"

"I'll explain everything, Brockey."

"Where'll we go?"

"Ter a quiet crib dat I knows about."

"Is it far?"

"No."

The two men arose from the table and hurried out of the saloon.

Carter was playing a dangerous game.

Would he be able to carry it through successfully to the end?

At any moment he was liable to make a slip and Brockey would then be able to penetrate his disguise.

So far he had deceived the rascal.

As they left the saloon the detective breathed easier. He had succeeded in getting Brockey away from his friends.

That was a great point gained.

They turned into Macdougal Street.

"Where are you goin'?" Brockey asked, after they had reached Fourth Street.

"Not far," Carter replied. "I've got a room around here in Fo'rt' Street."

"When did you hire it?"

"Ter-day."

"Oh!"

"Here it is."

The detective led the way into a private house.

Brockey's suspicions were not aroused.

If he had been aware that he was being led into a trap like a lamb to slaughter he would have then and there made a desperate fight.

Carter had rented a room in this house for years, and he had used it frequently. He opened the door of the room with a key.

The house was as quiet as a graveyard.

"This is a quiet joint," Brockey said, as he followed the detective into the room and gazed around.

There was nothing about the place to indicate for what purpose it had been used by the detective. It was nothing more, to all outward appearances, than a plainly furnished bedroom.

"Take a seat, Brockey," said Carter blandly, and at the same time he turned the key in the lock, took it out, and put it into his pocket.

"I wish you had some liquor about here," Brockey remarked, as he sank down into a chair.

"I kin accommodate youse."

"Can you?"

"Yes."

Carter opened a bureau drawer, took out a bottle and glasses and placed them on the table.

Brockey poured out a glassful of the liquor and drank it.

A few minutes after it was down a look of surprise spread over his face.

"Gosh!" he exclaimed. "Where did you get that, Mugsey?"

"Ain't it rich?" Carter asked, with a smile.

"It's more than rich."

"Where did you get it?"

"I swiped it off a drunk."

"I thought you didn't pay for it."

"Le' us talk bizness now."

Brockey's countenance changed. He leaned back in his chair, looked at the detective, and made no reply.

Carter was silent for a time, and then said:

"Brockey, as I said down in Samson's joint, I be on ter your game."

"And I'd like to know how you got on to it," Brockey growled.

"I'll tell youse after a while."

"Go ahead."

"Youse is mixed up in de Red Dragon Inn murder!"

"My Gawd!"

Brockey bounded out of his chair as if he had received a shock of electricity. His face was the color of ashes. He stood still and gasped at Carter.

"Youse needn't t'row a fit," the detective ejaculated. "Dere ain't no fly cop around here to hear me an' pinch youse."

"I'm a fool," Brockey exclaimed as he wiped the cold perspiration from his brow and sat down in his chair again.

"Rest easy, me covey."

"But, Mugsey, you puzzle me."

"Do I?"

"Yes."

Carter laughed.

"Fire ahead," Brockey said.

"Two rich blokes hired you to put Carter out o' de way.

"Un o' dem's named Darwin an' de oder Rich——"

"I——"

"Wait."

"I——"

"Es I said—dey hired youse, an' las' night youse broke into old Wright's room at de Cosmopolitan Hotel an' youse got sold."

"Mugsey——"

"Gi' me a chance to git through."

"I will."

"Now, I knows all dese tings, an' I know how much youse got—an' want a slice o' de dough, see?"

"And if I don't agree to give up?"

"Den I'll go to yer friend, Carter."

"You wouldn't do that?"

"Jess youse try ter t'row me down an' youse'll see wot I'll do."

"Mugsey——"

"Brockey, youse've got to come ter time."

"I suppose I'll have to."

"Youse kin gamble on dat."

"If I give up you'll have to help me."

"All right."

"I'll introduce you to Rich and Darwin."

"Tell me de full lay."

"Tell me how you got onto what you know."

"I piped youse."

"When?"

"Las' nite."

"Was that all?"

"Yes."

"Humph!"

"Doan git so disgusted."

"I'm not."

"Tell me de hull lay."

"I will."

Brockey became silent.

Carter's eyes sparkled as he watched his companion.

His heart was beating rapidly, but outwardly he appeared composed.

Patiently he waited for Brockey to commence to speak.

"Would the rascal speak the truth?" he asked himself.

Brockey was liable to tell a false story.

"I know more dan youse t'ink, Brockey," Carter remarked. "So if youse go ter givin' me any fairy tales I'll be down on youse wid all me force."

"I'm going to tell you all about the lay," Brockey replied, as he aroused himself out of his reverie.

"Den fire ahead."

"Don't get impatient."

"I'm not."

"Have you got anything to smoke?"

"Cert."

"Then set it out."

Carter placed some cigars on the table.

Brockey picked up one, lit it, and commenced to smoke.

With a sigh, he settled himself back in the chair.

Another silence followed, and it was nearly five minutes before he commenced to talk.

CHAPTER XII.
CAUGHT IN A TRAP.

"I want to tell you one thing, Mugsey," Brockey exclaimed suddenly, sitting bolt upright in his chair. "I'm not as deep in this affair of the Red Dragon Inn as you suspect."

"Don' gi' me any o' dat," Carter rejoined, blowing a cloud of smoke up in the air over his head.

"Upon my honor, what I tell you is the truth."

Carter could not help smiling when Brockey spoke of his honor.

Such a scoundrel as that does not know what honor is!

The detective knew well that Brockey had no honor, that he would lie, steal, and if he found himself in a tight place, he would not hesitate to betray an accomplice, if by so doing he could save himself.

Brockey noticed the smile, and he flared up instantly.

"What are you smiling at, Mugsey?" he demanded.

"Youse," Carter replied, without moving a muscle, and he puffed away at his cigar, unconcernedly.

"You are laughing at me?"

"Cert."

"I——"

"Youse gi' me a pain! Go on wid yer story."

"I want to know——"

"Drop it."

"What were you laughing at?"

"When *youse* talk o' honor it's 'nuff ter make a dorg laff."

"Is——"

"Come, Brockey—we's understand each udder—speel ahead, neider of us has got any honor, fur dat matter."

"All right."

Brockey quieted down. He took several pulls at his cigar, and then he continued:

"As I said, I'm not as deep in that Red Dragon Inn affair as you think."

"Let it go at dat."

"I'll tell you all about the affair, Mugsey.

"Then you and I can put our heads together and decide what to do."

"We'll gi' dem a good song and dance—make no mistake o' dat."

"How shall I start?"

"At de beginnin'."

"How else would I start?"

"Youse might start at de tail."

"That will do."

"Youse is wastin' time."

"Then keep quiet."

"I'm mum."

"Listen."

Brockey cleared his throat.

"It was the day before New Year's," he said.

"I was down on my luck and I hadn't a cent in my pocket.

"Not in a long time had I been in such a hole.

"I tried to touch a dozen o' the gang, but every one seemed to be in the same boat.

"No one could show me a cent.

"I was at Samson's saloon.

"Along about four o'clock a bloke came in.

"It was Sim Rich.

"Darwin had given me a knockdown to him some time before.

"At a glance I saw that he was excited about something.

"He spied me, came up, caught hold of my arm, dragged me after him out of the saloon, pushed me into a cab and ordered the cabby to hurry up and not lose sight of another cab that was just turning into Broadway.

"My breath was taken away.

"I didn't know what to make of Rich's actions.

"The cab started, and before I could utter a word, Rich said:

"'Brockey, I need your assistance.'

"'You can have it, if you pay for it,' I replied.

"'I'll pay,' Rich said.

"'Then what is it you want me to do?' I asked.

"'I want you to track a man.'

"Well, Rich pulled out a roll of bills and staked me with a hundred. He told me that in the cab which we were following was a man whom he hated and whom he wanted to locate.

"As soon as I found out where the man was going to put up I was to send him word.

"Rich got out of the cab.

"Before he did so he told me he was going to dine that night at the Knickerbocker Cottage, and I could send him word there."

"Why didn't Rich keep in wid youse?"

"He said he wanted to meet Darwin. He was in a very nervous condition, and another thing I saw that he had been drinking heavily.

"Well, he got out, and I kept on the bloke's trail.

"Finally the first cab stopped at the corner of Broadway and Sixteenth Street.

"My cab stopped on the next corner.

"I got out in a hurry, and I saw an old man get out of the other cab."

"Wot was de number of de cab youse was in?"

"Number one hundred and forty-seven."

"All right."

"As I said, an old man got out of the other cab. I got close up to him when he was paying the driver, and I heard him tell the man that he would not need him any longer.

"As the old bloke walked off I noticed that he had the lock step."

"You don't say!" interposed Nick.

"I do. At first I was not sure, but as I followed him and noted every action, I knew that he had been a guest at the big hotel up the river. He looked respectable enough, but there was the stamp of the prison on him.

"I followed the old fellow around all evening. He stopped in at a number of places and he seemed to be looking for some one.

"About ten o'clock he entered a restaurant on Sixth Avenue, and sat down at one of the tables.

"I went to the office of the district messenger company, wrote a note, and sent it to Rich, asking him to meet me at McKeever's place.

"In a short time he and Darwin met me in the saloon.

"We all had a drink.

"Then Rich listened to what I had to say about the old man.

"When we got outside of the saloon Rich said that he wouldn't need me any more that night, but he might the next day."

"And youse went off to blow in de hundred plunks?"

"Of course I did."

"Den youse don' know wot Rich an' Darwin did?"

"I surmise."

"Wot?"

"Rich and Darwin followed the old cove until they cornered him at the Red Dragon Inn."

"Yes."

"Then Rich got into the place and—you can imagine the rest."

"Youse don't know fer a certainty?"

"I didn't see it done."

"Was Rich familiar with the Red Dragon Inn?"

"Darwin told me that he used to go there years ago."

Carter had stopped using the tough vernacular, but Brockey did not notice it.

The detective was slightly disappointed. He thought at first that Brockey knew more about the crime. But still, the rascal's evidence would show that Rich and Darwin had said that they would follow the old man.

"Did Darwin tell you whether he or Rich followed the old man after you left them?" Carter asked.

"He did not," Brockey replied. "But I guess Rich was the one."

"What makes you think so?"

"Didn't you read about what the bartender had to say?"

"You mean about the tall man who entered the barroom after the old man?"

"Yes."

"Is that all you know?"

"It is, Mugsey."

"I think you know more."

"No."

Carter, while he was talking, rose from his chair, holding one of his hands in the side pocket of his coat.

Brockey did not move.

Even when the detective drew up near to him he did not suspect that he was in any danger. He poured out another glass full of liquor and drank it.

As he was in the act of placing the glass back on the table Carter caught hold of him, and, before he could move or utter a word, the detective had the handcuffs clasped around his wrists.

"What does this mean?" Brockey ejaculated, with a fierce oath, and, as he tried to jump to his feet, he faced the pistol which Carter pointed at him.

The detective pulled off his disguise.

Brockey recognized him. He uttered a cry of terror, his face turned pale with alarm, and he sank down into his chair.

"Carter!" he gasped.

"Yes, and you're my prisoner," the detective smilingly replied.

"I'm done for."

"There is not the slightest room for doubt, my dear Brockey."

"I never thought I'd be taken in in such a way—curse the luck!"

"There will be no chance for you to escape this time."

"If I had suspected——"

"You would have tried to have killed me."

"I would."

From his pocket Nick pulled out a silk cord.

With it he bound Brockey's arms and legs so tight that there was no chance for the rascal to escape.

"What are you going to do with me?" Brockey asked, when Carter had finished binding him.

"I am going to let you remain here for the present," the detective answered.

"Alone?"

"Oh, no!"

Brockey subsided into sullen silence, and glared fiercely at Carter.

Inwardly he cursed him.

The detective walked to the door and unlocked and opened it. Then he stepped out into the hall and gave a peculiar whistle.

In a few minutes Patsy bounded up the stairs from the floor below.

"What do you want, Mr. Carter?" the young man asked as he confronted his chief.

"I have a prisoner in that room," Carter replied, pointing toward the room. "I want you to guard him."

"I'll do it."

"See that you do, Patsy. If he should escape, my case might be ruined."

"He won't get a chance to escape."

"I hope not."

"Who is it?"

"Brockey Gann."

"Gee!"

"You know him?"

"I should say I do."

"He is a dangerous rascal."

"I'd like to have the honor of capturing him. I don't see how you accomplished it."

"I tricked him."

The young man entered the room and inspected Brockey.

Carter loitered outside in the hall for a few minutes and then he commenced to descend the stairs. He had considerable faith in his young assistant, and he was confident that Patsy would guard the prisoner as well as he would himself.

In that respect his mind was easy.

In the lower hall he made a few changes in his disguise and then he left the house.

He went up to the Grand Central Station and commenced to inspect the cabmen.

At last he found cab No. 147.

"Hello! How are you?"

The man looked at him for a moment and then exclaimed:

"Hello! How are ye?"

"Pretty well."

"Did you stick to the trail of that old bloke the other night?"

"Yes."

Carter had made himself up in such a manner that he looked like Brockey. He was delighted when the cabman recognized him as the thug.

"Who was he?" the cabby asked, after a silence.

"He was the man who was murdered at the Red Dragon Inn."

"You are joking!"

"I am not," protested Nick.

"I wouldn't like to stand in your shoes."

"Why not?"

"The fly cops'll get on to your following the old cove."

"They won't if you don't tell."

"I might make some money by telling."

"You won't do that?"

"Why shouldn't I?"

"You'll get an innocent man into a hole."

"That's so. But, I say, where's the tall mug?"

"Who do you mean?"

"I mean the man who employed me."

"I thought you knew him?"

"No, I don't," said the cabman. "He just picked me up here at the depot and he ordered me to follow the other mug."

"I thought he was a detective."

"You know who he is?"

"Honestly, I do not."

"Would you call on him if I should give you his name and address?"

"Of course, I would."

"What will you do?"

"I'll make him come down with the rocks."

"Will you whack up with me?"

"Of course I will."

"You'll play square?"

"I swear it."

"His name is Simeon Rich, and he lives in the Studio Building, at the corner of Broadway and Thirty-first Street."

"Gosh!"

"What are you going to do?"

"I'm going to get some one to mind my rig and I'm going to call on Mr. Rich."

"I'll see you downtown."

Carter hurried away. He stopped at a saloon and made a change in his disguise in the back room.

When he came out he was just in time to see cabby No. 147 making a bee line down Park Avenue. He started after him.

What object had Carter in view when he gave Rich's name and address to the cabman?

CHAPTER XIII.
BLACKMAIL.

The cabman did not allow the grass to grow under his feet.

It did not take him long to reach the Studio Building.

"He's a rascal," Carter commented, as he tracked the cabman; "I can make use of him."

The detective was amused.

That he had formulated some shrewd move was quite certain from the manner in which he was acting.

The cabman entered the Studio Building.

Carter was close behind him.

Not for an instant did the man suspect that he was the person who had given Rich's name and address to him.

"Does Mr. Rich live here?" the cabman asked of the elevator boy.

Carter was standing in the elevator, and he heard what was said.

"Mr. Rich lives on the top floor," the boy replied to the cabman.

"Is he in?" the cabman inquired, getting into the elevator.

"You can go up and see."

"All right."

When the top floor was reached the elevator boy pointed out Rich's room.

The cabman hurried up and knocked on the door.

Carter walked leisurely down the hall. He halted halfway down and looked out of the window. He stood in such a position that he was able to see the cabby.

Three times the driver pounded on the door without receiving a response.

The fourth time he knocked as if he were going to break in a panel.

Some one opened the door.

Carter could not see who it was from where he was standing, but he heard the cabman exclaim:

"I want to see Mr. Simeon Rich."

"He isn't in," a female voice replied.

Carter did not recognize it, but he surmised that it belonged to either Sally Rich or Isabella Porter.

"I want to see him, miss," the cabby insolently said. "If he isn't in I'll wait until he comes."

"Who are you?" the woman within the room asked.

"It doesn't matter who I am."

"It doesn't, eh? Well, I guess it does."

"Is Rich in there? If he is, tell him that the cabman who drove him about town on the day before New Year's wants to see him."

"Let him come in," a man's voice called out from the interior of the room.

The coachman pushed by the woman and entered the apartment.

Instantly the door was closed.

Carter hurried up to the door.

A transom was above it.

It was halfway open.

Reaching up, Carter caught hold of the edge of the sill under the transom and pulled himself up until he was able to peer into the room. He beheld Rich and Darwin seated on divans at the side, and two women lolling back in steamer chairs. The cabman was standing in the center of the apartment gazing boldly at Rich.

"What do you want?" Rich demanded, in a stern tone, as he glared at the cabby.

"Do you want me to talk out before these people?" the cabby asked, looking around the room at those present and waving his hand toward them.

"I have no secrets from them."

"You haven't, eh?"

"No."

"Then you must all be in the same boat. This is rich graft."

"What do you mean?"

Rich uttered an oath and sprang up. He realized that the cabby knew something. He was enough of a student of human nature to read the man's intentions in the expression of his face.

The cabman did not flinch.

"I guess you'll come to time, Mr. Rich," he insolently remarked, with a sneer.

Rich stood within a few feet of him. He raised his arm above his head, as if he intended to strike the man, but thinking better of it, he allowed it to drop to his side again, and he muttered an oath.

Cabby was no fool. He knew what was in Rich's mind.

"If you had tried to strike me then I'd have floored you," he growled. "And it is well for you that you did not try it on."

Rich made no reply. He only glared at the cabby in silence.

His face was as dark as night.

Carter hung on to the sill. He had viewed the scene through the transom, and he had heard every word that had been uttered.

His arms were aching. He was forced to let go his hold.

Without making a noise he dropped to the floor.

Now he stood outside the door and listened.

At last he heard Rich exclaim:

"Speak out, sir, and tell me how you learned my name and address?"

"I'm not giving my friends away," the cabby replied.

"What do you want?"

"Money."

"Money!"

"Yes."

"What for?"

"To keep my tongue from wagging."

"I——"

"You understand me, Mr. Rich. The man whom you tracked from the Grand Central on the day before New Year's was the man who was murdered at the Red Dragon Inn."

Carter had raised himself up again so that he was peering through the transom when the cabman uttered these words.

Rich did not start. He displayed not the least sign of fear. He glanced at the man with a sinister expression upon his darkly handsome face.

"I am aware of that," he replied, in cold, harsh tones.

"You are a good bluffer, Rich," the cabby remarked, and he smiled.

It was as good as looking at a play to watch these two men.

Both now had their tempers under command.

"You call me a bluffer," Rich retorted.

"I do," cabby rejoined. "I am not afraid of you. I will go to the police and inform them that you tracked Lawrence on the day before New Year's, and you hired one of the worst thugs in the city to keep on his trail. Carter would reward me liberally for this information."

"You are a scoundrelly blackmailer."

"I acknowledge the corn. I've got you in a corner and you will have to pay——"

"Not one cent will I give you."

"Think twice, Mr. Rich."

"Be careful, Sim."

It was one of the women who spoke. She had come up to Rich's side and laid her hand gently upon his arm.

The man glanced at her and said:

"I know what I am about, Sally."

Carter knew from this that the woman was Rich's sister. The other woman he surmised was Isabella Porter.

A broad grin spread over the cabby's face.

"Yes, be careful, Mr. Rich," he sneered. He was becoming more insolent the longer he waited.

Rich wheeled around. His large, black eyes were flashing, his face was aflame with passion.

"*You* be careful," he hissed between his clenched, white teeth, and he drew his arm back.

Sally threw herself between her brother and the cabman.

"Sim," she ejaculated, "calm yourself."

"Yes, calm yourself, my covey," cabby repeated with a chuckle.

Rich bit the ends of his mustache and glared. He was making a desperate effort to keep calm. A silence followed.

Cabby kept his eyes on Rich.

When he saw that Simeon was not going to speak he said:

"Let us get down to business, Rich. There is no use of trying to bluff me. I'm too old a bird to stand any kind of a jolly.

"I can read your character, and you ought to be able to read mine.

"If I should go to the police with the information which I possess, you know they would come down on you heavily."

"Wait one moment."

"Let me finish.

"I have no desire to injure you if you treat me halfway decently.

"Times have been very bad with me lately, and I need money.

"I feel convinced that you and your friends have gained by the death of old Lawrence.

"In to-day's paper was published an account of the Lawrence will case, and it was suggested that a search be made for you and the wife and daughter of the murdered man.

"The police do not know where you are.

"They have no evidence against you.

"But I can furnish that evidence.

"Now, how much is it worth to you for me to keep silent?"

The cabby spoke calmly and deliberately. Rich followed him closely. He frowned, and his fingers worked nervously, as if he were desiring to spring upon the man and strangle him. He did not reply for some moments. He looked around at Darwin and the women.

"What shall I do?" was in his eyes.

"Pay," Darwin said, alarmed.

Rich turned his eyes on the cabman.

"How much do you want?" he asked.

"One thousand dollars," cabby coolly replied, without changing an expression.

"Absurd!"

"No, it is not."

"It is."

"To keep me quiet one thousand dollars is a small sum."

"How do I know, if I do pay you this sum, that you will not give me away, anyhow?"

"I never go back on my word."

"I will give you five hundred."

"Not a cent less than a thousand."

"I can't give you any such sum as that to-day."

"I won't be hard on you."

"Thank you."

"You don't mean that. I'll take part on account."

"I'll give you one hundred."

"Make it three."

"I can't, I tell you."

"I'll take the century."

"Here it is."

"Now, when will you pay the balance?"

"To-morrow."

"Shall I call here?"

"No; I will send the money to you."

"At my stand?"

"Yes."

"What time?"

"Noon."

"Very well."

"It'll be on hand."

"See that it is."

"What is your name?"

"Pete McCree."

"What is the number of your cab?"

"Number one hundred and forty-seven."

Cabby started toward the door.

Before he turned around, Carter dropped. He ran toward the elevator, which he reached before the door of the room was opened.

While standing with his back turned he changed his disguise.

Then he got into the elevator.

As soon as the detective reached the street he halted near the entrance.

When McCree came out he walked up to him and tapped him on the shoulder.

"Hello!" McCree ejaculated.

"I'm on hand," Carter remarked.

"So I see."

"How much did you get?"

"Not much."

"How much?"

"One hundred bones."

"Why didn't you make him pay more?"

"He couldn't produce to-day, but he will do so to-morrow."

"I get half."

"Certainly."

"You are square."

"I'll get this note changed."

"I'll change it."

"Have you got fifty?"

"Yes."

"Here's the century."

Carter took the bill and handed the cabby back fifty dollars.

"Now let me give you a piece of advice," he said.

"What is it?" McCree asked.

"Keep out of risky places to-night and be on your guard."

"Why?"

"You are dealing with desperate men."

"I am aware of that, pard."

"Rich may employ some one to try and put you out of the way."

"You should have seen how he acted."

"I can imagine what he said."

"I'd like to know what kind of a game he and those others are playing?"

"So would I."

"I've got to get back to the stand. I'll see you to-morrow."

Carter shook hands with the rascally cabman, and they separated. The detective hastened away.

Half an hour later he was ushered into the presence of the cashier of the safe deposit company.

"Have you discovered a clew?" the cashier asked.

"I'll reply to that question as soon as you have answered a few queries which I am going to put to you," the detective said.

"What is it?"

"You said that you gave Mr. Lawrence new bills."

"I did."

"Do you remember the numbers?"

"I can tell you in a moment."

The cashier walked over to a desk, picked up a slip of paper, referred to it and said:

"They were from 177865B to 177870B."

"Keno!" Carter shouted. He held in his hand the note which Rich had given to the cabman. He was looking at it when the cashier read the numbers.

"What is the matter?" the cashier asked.

"Do you see this bill?" Carter said, as he held the bill out for the cashier to inspect.

"Gracious! Captain, that note is numbered one hundred and seventy-seven thousand eight hundred and sixty-nine B! That is one of the bills which I gave to Mr. Lawrence!"

"Will you swear to that?"

"I will. That is one of the bills."

"Thank you."

The two men were silent.

CHAPTER XIV.
TIGHTENING THE COILS.

The cashier of the safe deposit company kept gazing in silence at Carter with open-mouthed astonishment.

Nick's countenance was illumined with an expression of triumph. He held in his hand damaging evidence against Simeon Rich.

If Rich were innocent of the murder, how was it that he had in his possession one of the bills which the cashier of the safe deposit company had paid to the man who had been so cruelly murdered at the Red Dragon Inn?

"This is a valuable clew," the detective said, when the silence was becoming oppressive.

"How did that bill come into your possession?" the cashier asked.

"I think you can keep a secret?"

"I can."

"Then I will tell you."

Then Carter gave the cashier a short account of the evidence which he had collected.

When the detective finished the cashier remarked:

"Captain, you are gradually weaving the coils around Simeon Rich."

"Yes," Carter replied, "I am weaving coils around him, but I have no positive evidence that he committed the crime."

"That note?"

"Not positive. If he has others of the series in his possession, then the coil will be stronger around him."

"I understand. What move will you make next?"

"I cannot determine just now."

Carter was elated over the discovery.

After leaving the cashier's office he went direct to the house on Fourth Street.

Here he found that Brockey was still a prisoner.

His young assistant was on guard.

"Brockey," said the detective, as he stood in front of the prisoner, "have you spent all the money that Darwin gave you?"

"What's that to you?" Brockey snarled, being in an ugly mood.

And no wonder!

Who could blame him?

Brockey was by no means a stoic or a philosopher. His was a nature which would brood on troubles.

There was bitter hatred and malice in every flash of his eye. No love there, no appreciation of the detective's ability!

Carter gazed down into that dark countenance. He read the man's thoughts.

"If you have any of that money left," Carter replied, in a serious tone, "some of it may be bills which were stolen from the murdered man."

"I have the numbers of those bills in my possession."

Instantly the expression on Brockey's face changed.

A look of terror came over it.

It had not occurred to him before that the money might have belonged to the man who was killed at the Red Dragon Inn.

"Do you understand?" Carter asked at length, when Brockey made no reply.

"I understand," the rascal said, with a gasp.

"If you should have one of those bills on you, and if it should be identified as belonging to Lawrence, then, if I were so inclined, I could fix the murder on you."

"You would not do that?"

"No, I would not."

"I have some of the money."

"Is it in your pocket?"

"Yes."

Carter put his hand into Brockey's trousers pocket and pulled out a small roll of bills. He ran the money over and found one of the series.

"This is one," he remarked, holding the bill up for Brockey to inspect.

"My God!" the rascal ejaculated.

"You will have to tell now in court how this came into your possession."

"I'll tell quick enough."

"I guess you will."

"Let me look at the number."

"See?"

"I do."

The rest of the money the detective gave to Brockey.

The bill he marked and put away in his pocketbook with the others.

The evidence against Rich was stronger.

But still more evidence was needed before a case could be proven.

Carter left the house.

Slowly he walked through to Broadway, and when he reached that thoroughfare he halted on the corner and reviewed the events of the past few days. He was forced to acknowledge in spite of himself that the evidence against Simeon Rich was strong.

But still he was not satisfied.

Dora Ferris' testimony and that of Lena Peters would be damaging.

The testimony of the cashier, the cabman, and Brockey would be sensational.

And the note which he had found in Darwin's room in Dora's flat would tighten the coil.

But it was not enough.

"Every link in the chain of evidence must be complete," Carter muttered. What move ought he to make?

"Should he close in on Rich and his pals and take the chance of discovering the needed evidence against them?"

"No, I won't do that," the detective muttered, as this question flashed through his mind.

He turned and wended his way uptown.

It was seven o'clock when he halted in front of the Studio Building.

Some force seemed to impel him to enter. He did not go near the elevator; but he walked upstairs to the top floor. He strolled along the hall and stopped in front of the door of Rich's room.

No light shone through the transom.

Were the conspirators out?

Carter knocked.

No one came to the door.

"They must have gone out," he muttered.

At the same time he pulled a skeleton key out of his pocket and inserted it in the lock of the door.

Two quick turns of the key and the bolt of the lock slipped back.

Carter entered the room, and struck a match.

As the flame flickered up, and after he had looked around, he uttered an exclamation of surprise.

Around him were all the evidences of hasty flight.

The birds had flown.

Carter lit the gas.

Then he was able to make an inspection.

A look of chagrin rested upon his face as his eyes wandered around the room.

The furniture belonging to the room of the building was not disturbed.

The floor was strewn with rubbish.

After the detective recovered from his surprise he commenced to make a search of the apartment. He rooted among the scraps of paper on the floor in the hope that he would find something of value.

He made no discovery.

Every bureau drawer was gone through.

Nothing.

At last Carter made a search of the two closets.

Result?

Nothing.

He stood in the center of the room thinking.

His eyes wandered around.

Was there any evidence in that room? He asked the question over and over again.

He was confident that his search had been most thorough. But had it been? Was there not some place about that room which contained evidence, and which had escaped the eagle eyes of the visitor?

Carter suddenly started.

"The fireplace!" he ejaculated, and he sprang forward.

At that moment his eyes had fallen on some soot which covered the carpet in front of the fireplace.

What did this indicate? He had not examined the fireplace!

Down upon his knees he fell in front of the grate.

Up into the chimney he thrust his hand and arm.

The next instant he pulled out a large bundle.

A cloud of soot fell down, and the detective was covered with it.

He paid no attention to it.

All of his thoughts were on that bundle, which he carried over to the center of the room.

Slowly he unwound the wrapper.

Then a long ulster was disclosed.

Carter shook out the folds.

A black slouch hat and a false beard fell to the floor.

Was it any wonder that the detective's hands shook as he gazed upon and held this evidence?

He examined the ulster.

Down the front were a number of dark stains.

Upon the right sleeve was a large dark splash as large as a man's hand.

"Blood!" Carter ejaculated, as he inspected these stains.

He looked inside the ulster at the stamp on the strap.

"Made by Delaney," he read.

"This was made to order," he muttered.

"For whom?"

That was the question.

"I'll find out!" he ejaculated, after a moment's thought.

Down into the pockets of this ulster his hand was shoved.

One after the other was turned inside out.

Not a scrap of paper could he find.

All the outside pockets had been gone through.

Then Carter turned his attention to those inside.

"Nothing!" he muttered.

It was disappointing.

But the detective was not downcast. He picked up the slouch hat and the beard, and examined them.

Inside the beard was stamped the word Dazian.

"That's the name of the costumer," Carter muttered, as he read that name.

There were no marks inside the hat.

The lining had been torn out.

The ulster and the hat the detective tied up in a bundle, and the false beard he put into his pocket.

For a few minutes longer he remained in the room searching, but he made no further discovery.

Taking the evidence under his arm, he left the apartment.

It was an important discovery. He felt sure that he had in his possession the ulster worn by the murderer when he committed the crime.

In going down in the elevator the detective questioned the boy in charge.

The boy said that Rich and Darwin had moved out just at dusk, and they did not say where they were going.

Carter stopped at the office, and the clerk was not able to give him any information.

When he left the Studio Building he was perfectly calm. He did not seem to be disturbed about the sudden departure of the men.

The thought that they might have left the city did not enter his mind.

Carter crossed Broadway to the little park in front of the bank building.

Here he moved about among the cabmen making inquiries.

All claimed that they had not taken any fares from the Studio Building.

From Greeley Square the detective walked across to the opposite corner, where a solitary express wagon was standing.

The man in charge was partly intoxicated.

"Did you cart away anything from the Studio Building this evening?" Carter asked as he came up to the man.

"You may bet I did," the man blurted out in thick tones. "I made a good stake."

"They were nice men?"

"You may bet they were."

"Where did you leave the things?"

"In a flat at number two hundred and forty-one West Thirty-sixth Street."

"What name?"

"Lawrence."

"Are you sure that was the name?"

"Of course I am. The tall fellow wrote it down on a slip of paper for me."

"Was he at the flat to receive the things?"

"No. The two ladies were there, though."

"Only the two ladies?"

"That was all."

Carter did not go direct to the address on West Thirty-sixth Street after he left the expressman. He hurried down to Union Square and entered Dazian's musty-smelling establishment.

To the clerk in charge he showed the false beard.

"We made that," the clerk said, after he had examined the disguise.

"Do you remember selling a beard like that lately?" the detective asked.

"I remember selling this."

"You do?"

"Yes."

"When did you sell it?"

"The morning of the day before New Year's."

"To whom did you sell it?"

"A tall man."

"Did you sell him anything else?"

"Yes."

"What?"

"A Moorish dagger."

"Anything else?"

"No."

"Did he give you his name?"

"No. He paid for the things and he took them away with him."

"What kind of a coat had he on?"

"An ulster."

"What kind of a hat?"

"An old slouch."

"Is this the color of the ulster?"

Carter untied the bundle while he was talking, and now he displayed the ulster in front of the clerk.

"It was that color," the young man ejaculated. "And that is the slouch hat. I remember noticing that the rim was slightly torn."

"Would you be able to identify that man?"

"I would."

"Was he alone?"

"Yes."

The detective next went to the tailoring establishment conducted by Delaney. He showed the ulster to the manager.

"We made that garment six years ago," the manager said, after he had inspected the coat.

"Can you tell for whom?" Carter asked. "If you can tell me, I shall be greatly obliged."

"I can. Do you notice this number in indelible ink on the pocket flap? Well, that is the number of the order. I will refer to our books."

He walked back into the office and examined a large ledger.

In a few moments he returned to Carter and said:

"That coat was made for a gentleman named Simeon Rich."

"Thank you," Carter rejoined, and then he departed.

The coils around Rich were tightening, but the detective had not found that weapon with which the crime had been committed.

Perhaps the murderer had thrown it away.

That was likely.

That the weapon was a Moorish dagger and the one purchased at Dazian's the detective was convinced.

On a mere whim, Nick took all his evidence down to police headquarters and made a report to the chief inspector.

When he was through the chief said:

"I will send out men to fetch in all the witnesses.

"We will assemble them here in this room, and then, if we corral the conspirators, we will bring them in. Mark my word. We will get a confession from one of them."

"I'll make out a list of the witnesses."

"Call them off and I'll write them down."

"The bartender at the Red Dragon Inn, Doctor Thompson, Peter Wright, Brockey Gann, Lena Peters, Lem Samson, Dora Ferris, Dazian's clerk, the cashier of the safe deposit company, Delaney's manager, and the cabman, number one hundred and forty-seven."

"I'll send out men for them."

"Very well."

"What are you going to do?"

"Close in on Rich."

"Do you need assistance?"

"Give me two men."

The chief inspector called in two men and they went out with Carter.

They entered a taxicab and were driven to the address given to the detective by the expressman.

The name of Lawrence was on the letter box belonging to the first flat.

Carter entered the hall with his men.

One of them he sent back to guard the back door of the flat and prevent escape by that exit. Then he knocked on the front door, which was opened by a tall, comely, gray-haired woman.

Within he heard voices.

"What do you want?" the woman asked, as Carter and his aid shoved past her.

The detective made no reply. He and his companion darted into the parlor.

Rich and Darwin and three women were there.

All sprang to their feet.

The women screamed.

Carter covered the men with his revolver and exclaimed:

"Rich, there is no chance for you to escape. The house is surrounded by my men. You may as well submit quietly."

"What does this intrusion mean?" Rich demanded.

"It means that I arrest you for the murder of Alfred Lawrence, and these others"—looking around the room at the others and pausing for a moment—"I arrest them as your accomplices."

In a short time the two men were manacled.

They offered no resistance, because they saw that it would be of no avail.

The two detectives guarded the prisoners while Carter made a search of the flat.

In a trunk belonging to Rich he found a Moorish dagger, the blade and hilt of which were stained with blood. He also found an old pocketbook with papers belonging to the murdered man in it.

On this were marks of bloody fingers.

The woman who admitted Carter was the wife of the murdered man, and the third woman in the parlor was Lawrence's daughter. She was a beautiful young woman, but at a glance the detective saw that she had been leading a life of dissipation.

The prisoners were taken to police headquarters.

When Rich was led into the chief inspector's office and he beheld the witnesses congregated there all his bravado fled.

"The game is up!" he ejaculated, and he sank into a chair, his handsome face the color of death. "You cornered me, Mr. Carter. I killed Lawrence. There is no use for me to deny anything. When I learned that he was about to be released from Sing Sing I made up my mind to kill him. I feared him, and so did his wife. I knew there was evidence in existence to prove that we had conspired against him.

"I suppose you have received statements from all these people and there is no use for me to make a long confession.

"All I'll say will be that I tracked Lawrence to the Red Dragon Inn, and when the bartender's back was turned I slipped upstairs and hid in the parlor.

"Then I waited until the house was quiet, when I stole up to Lawrence's room and killed him.

"I escaped through the window and then down the ladder to the back yard.

"I solemnly swear that Mrs. Lawrence and her daughter had nothing to do with the crime."

The mystery of the Red Dragon Inn was solved at last, and when the newspapers published the facts in regard to the work done by Carter a sensation was created. Nick had little time to bask in the glow of journalistic applause, even had he cared to do so. He was soon plunged in the case to which his assistants had been paving his way by their investigations.

CHAPTER XV.
MURDER IN HELL'S KITCHEN.

To understand the preliminaries of the case on which Chick Carter and Patsy had been working for their chief, we must go back to a time before Simeon Rich was tried and executed, before Darwin was sent back to England, where he afterward died in prison.

To begin with, Old Mother Flintstone, well known in the neighborhood of Hell's Kitchen, was dead.

All people have to die, and the old woman had to follow the written law of all mankind; but, what was queer, her death was a subject for police investigation.

She had not lived the best of lives, this old hag, toothless and decrepit in her hovel, where her couch was rags and the walls grimy and almost black; she had been a fence and what not, and there were stories about her that made people even in that delectable quarter of Gotham shake their heads over them.

She had died in the night.

Death had come to the hovel in the wee sma' hours of the darkness, when the great city was supposed to sleep the sleep of the innocent and righteous; but somehow or other there was a suspicion that a human hand had helped Mother Flintstone out of the world.

She lived alone, but now and then she was visited by a boy—a waif of the streets, little, but shrewd and wiry.

Mulberry Billy, as the boy was called, had a story to tell, and it was his narrative which had set the police agog.

The boy had gone to Mother Flintstone's just before day, crawling into the old place, where he knew there was always a bed for him, and had found the old lady lying on her face on the floor.

Billy tried to lift the body and bear it to the couch near by, but the lot of bones slid from his hands.

Then he saw the distorted face, the wide, staring eyes and the clenched hands.

Then he saw that his old benefactress was past all human aid, and he stood stock-still and thought how kind she had been to him.

But this was not all Billy saw. He was attracted to the right by a noise in the direction of the only window in the room, and there he saw the outlines of a face.

It was not a rough face, as one would expect to see in that locality; it was not the face of a hardened ruffian, seamed with sin and desperate. It was a finely cut face, handsome, aristocratic, like those Billy sometimes saw on Fifth Avenue or Broadway. It had good eyes, white skin, a broad forehead, and well-chiseled lips. The mustache did not entirely hide the latter, but it did not let the boy get a good look at them.

If the face at the window had been wicked-looking or desperate the boy would not have been astonished, for he would have thought that the desperate murderer had come back to see if the victim had yet been discovered.

Mother Flintstone was reputed rich; she was said to have accumulated by her calling a good deal of wealth, which she had concealed somewhere, but where even Billy, her one little confidant, did not know.

The boy looked at the face till it seemed to be photographed on his mind. He would know it among a thousand faces, he thought.

It should not escape him, and he would give a certain person a full description of it.

In a moment, as it were, the face vanished.

Billy turned again to the dead woman, but looked now and then toward the window. He saw that the old woman had been killed, for the rent in her throat told where the dagger had found her life and put an end to her varied career.

As yet the murder was his secret and the murderer's.

Mulberry Billy remained in the little room some time, or until he had composed his nerves.

One does not discover a terrible crime every day, not even in New York. He wanted to think the matter over a little; he wanted to decide just what to do.

"I'll see Patsy again, that's best," he said aloud, though addressing himself. "Patsy Garvan once befriended me, and he'll tell Mr. Carter about this, and I know Mr. Carter's the man to take charge of this matter and avenge Mother Flintstone."

With this the street Arab slipped from the house and went out upon the street again.

In a few minutes he ran up a flight of steps leading to Nick's downtown den, where he had captured Brockey, and knocked at a door.

Footsteps crossed the room beyond and the door was opened.

"You, boy! Come in."

Billy entered, looking at the person who had opened the door, and who now stood in the middle of the room looking at him with a smile on his face. He had expected to find Chick Carter or Patsy there, and he was surprised to meet the great detective himself already on the trail once more.

"What's happened, boy?" asked Nick.

"They've got Mother Flintstone at last, sir."

"Who have?"

"That's for you to find out, Mr. Carter."

"You don't mean that the old lady's dead, Billy?"

"Don't I?"

"Where?"

"In the crib."

"Do you know who saw her last?"

"Yes, sir; the man who did it."

Carter smiled at the answer and took a seat at the table.

"Give me the story," he said.

Billy did so. He omitted nothing, but he dwelt a long time on the face at the window.

The famous detective seemed to think that face an important matter, and he made the boy describe it half a dozen times.

Presently he arose and put on an overcoat, for the night was cold, and perhaps he wanted to protect his face with the ample collar.

The pair left the room together, and Billy piloted the detective to the scene of the crime.

"You can go now," said Carter, when he had taken a survey of the apartment. "I will need you to-morrow, Billy. Don't go far. You can take my lounge if you want a snooze till then."

The urchin went away, leaving Carter in the hovel where Mother Flintstone lay.

Nick went over the old place with his keen eyes and eager hands.

If he found anything that let some light upon the mystery he did not divulge the secret, and just as day was breaking over the spires of Gotham he came out of the place and walked away.

A few minutes later the police knew of the crime, and a sergeant took possession of the old woman's abode.

Hell's Kitchen had a new sensation, and its inhabitants stood about in groups and discussed it.

The sensation was too late for the morning papers, but it would do for the afternoon journals; and as Mother Flintstone was a noted character, half a dozen reporters came to the scene with ready pencils and reportorial noses.

The papers in the afternoon told all there was to tell.

They dished up the past life of the old woman and colored it to suit themselves.

Some had her a woman once respected and wealthy, the wayward daughter of a money king; others said she was related to royalty; none put her down as plain Mother Flintstone—that, you know, being the unvarnished truth, would never do!

The wasted body was removed to the morgue and the surgeons brought their skill to bear upon the case. All agreed that the old creature had been foully killed by a dagger, and the coroner's jury added "by some person unknown," and then turned the matter over to the police.

The following night Carter, alone in his room, heard a rap on his door, and he opened it to look into the face of a young woman. He held the door open and the girl—she was no more than this in years—glided into the room.

"Lock the door, please," she said, with an appealing look at the detective.

Carter did so and turned to her.

His visitor had taken a chair, and in the light he saw how frightened she was and how she trembled.

"You haven't any clew yet?" was her first question.

"Clew to what?"

"Why, to the murderer of Mother Flintstone."

"Oh, you're interested in that, are you?"

"I am."

"What is your name?"

"Yes, I thought you'd want to know that and it's no more than right that I should tell you. You may call me Margie Marne."

"But that's not your name."

The girl smiled.

"Perhaps not; don't, for Heaven's sake, rob me of the only secret I have—my true identity."

"I will not. You shall keep your name. That secret can belong to you as long as you want it, or until you see best to disclose it."

"The time may come when I can speak," was the reply. "But you haven't answered my question yet."

"About the clew? It's a queer case."

"And a dark one?"

"Yes."

"No reward has been offered?"

"Not a dollar."

"But you want to find out who killed Mother Flintstone, and why."

"I do, and I will find out."

"Thank God!" cried Margie Marne, rising from her chair and seizing Carter's hands. "That's the best thing I ever heard a man say."

"What was the old lady to you?"

"Don't ask me. Only find the hand that slew her."

"That's my mission, as I've already told you."

"I'll reward you," and she seemed to smile again. "I don't look like a person of wealth, but I can reward the man who solves this mystery of the tenements. I'm not as poor as I look, not a female Lazarus by any means."

"You don't look it, either."

The girl would have replied if footsteps had not approached the detective's door, and he crossed the room.

Billy, the street Arab, bounded in the moment the door was opened.

"I've located him!" he cried the moment he caught sight of Carter. "I can show you the face I saw at the window last night. Come! Let the gal stay. We don't want her. No gals in the case for Mulberry Billy is my motto," and the boy darted toward the door again.

CHAPTER XVI.
THE MILLIONAIRE'S GUEST.

In another part of the city about the same time that witnessed these events a scene was being enacted which is destined to have an important bearing on Carter's present case of mystery.

This time it was not in the heart of that tough locality called Hell's Kitchen, but in the haunts of the better classes, indeed, in what might be called the abode of wealth.

Perry Lamont was a multimillionaire. He was a man of past fifty, but with very few gray hairs and a florid complexion. He was not engaged in any business, having retired from the "Street" some years prior to the opening of our story, and now was resting at his ease.

Surrounded with wealth of every description, this man was an envied person and a man to be congratulated on the easy life he could lead in his luxurious mansion.

Blessed with wife and children, the latter grown to manhood and womanhood, he passed his days in luxury, his only fad being fast horses, with which his stables were filled.

Perry Lamont sat in the splendid library of his home and smoked a prime cigar. He was alone. His wife and daughter had gone to the opera and his son was playing billiards at the club.

Therefore Lamont had the whole house to himself, for it was the servants' night off, and he had resolved to take his ease.

Suddenly the clear tones of the bell reverberated through the mansion, but the millionaire did not rise. He did not want any visitors, and he was not at all in the humor to be disturbed.

Again the bell rang, a little sharper than before, and he laid down the cigar.

"Confound it all, why can't a fellow get a little rest?" he growled, crossing the room toward the hall.

"It's a pity some people haven't the slightest notion about propriety, but must come when a man wants to throw off the cares of the world and enjoy himself."

For the third time the bell jangled, and the next moment Lamont reached the door. He opened it with a growl on his lips, but all at once a man rudely pushed past him into the hall.

"Good evening," said the stranger, who was tall and decidedly good looking from what the millionaire could see of his face, for he kept his collar up. "Don't think I'm an intruder. Of course, I came here on business, and that overleaps every other consideration, you know."

"Business? This way, then."

Lamont led the way to the library, where he waved his caller to a chair.

"You have a son, I believe?" said the visitor.

"I have. I guess that's no disgrace," smiled Perry Lamont, who was inordinately proud of his son and heir.

"He's at the club just now?"

"That's his pleasure, I suppose."

"Certainly. Is he your only son?"

"He is."

"And you look to him to keep up the honor of the house of Lamont?"

"He'll do that, never fear, Claude will."

"That is, he will if the law will let him."

The nabob started.

"Have a care, sir!" he cried, coloring. "This is my house, and a man's house is his castle."

"That's old, but good," grinned the unwelcome and uncivil caller. "I've often wondered where that saying originated, but never had time to look it up."

Lamont looked at the man amazed, for he never saw such coolness in all his life.

"You've got a daughter, too," continued the stranger.

"What's that to you?"

"Not much, perhaps, but a good deal to you."

"There you're right; but you shall not make sport of my child. My affection for her is too sacred for that."

"She's pretty and good. I know her."

"*You?*" almost roared the millionaire, falling back in his chair and staring at the other. "This is carrying a joke too far."

"Just as you think; but let's go back to Claude."

"No, I won't have another thing to do with you. You remember you are not an invited guest——"

"That's right—not an invited guest, but I don't quit this house till I care to go."

"By Jove——"

"Come, come, keep your temper."

"You won't let me," said Lamont, with a faint smile.

"Well, this boy of yours is a little wild. He's the lion of the club, but he don't always keep within the bounds of the law."

"How?"

"I don't mean to insinuate anything, only to remind you that he is just now harvesting his crop of wild oats."

"Just as far too as many boys do."

"But the yield is larger on some grounds than on others."

"You don't mean——"

"That your hopeful is reaping a gorgeous crop, eh? That's it precisely."

"But he knows when to stop."

"The sheriff will do that."

Lamont started forward, and for the first time his face became really pale.

"That's an insult!"

"I thought you would consider it such."

"It is infamous!"

"You're good at words."

"Come, this interview is at an end."

"Not yet. What will you give to save your son?"

"To save him? He's committed no crime yet——"

"Will you give ten thousand?"

"Not a dollar! If Claude has committed some little indiscretion such as young men will——"

"He's done more than that. It would be charity to designate it by the name you have just mentioned, but the authorities would call it something else."

"Where is Claude?"

"At the club, just where you said he was."

"Then——"

"I'll take ten thousand and save the boy."

"From what?"

"The electric chair!"

Perry Lamont seemed to reel in his chair, and it was with difficulty that he kept his seat.

"It's a lie!" he cried.

"Just as you like. It's all true, however."

"It's false, I say, as false as perdition! My boy wouldn't stoop to crime."

"No; he's an angel. And all he wants is a pair of wings which would just fix him out."

Lamont reddened and then turned pale again.

"I announce this interview terminated," he said, but his voice was agitated and his gaze wandered to the door across the room.

"You can write out the check for the amount I have mentioned if you have any regard for the honor of your house."

"Not a dollar!"

"Then take the consequences!"

So threatening, the man arose and coolly buttoned his coat.

"You're mad," said the millionaire.

"Perhaps. I'm money mad, but I want to save you and yours. I don't want to heap disgrace upon your wife and daughter. I don't want to disgrace you and see your boy go to the chair. I don't want to do anything of the kind, and I won't if you pay me for the secret."

Perhaps something told Perry Lamont that he was dealing with a desperate man, who, after all, might have the secret he spoke of, but it was such a terrible thing to think of that it chilled his blood.

"I'm a man of business. I want the check or your boy is exposed."

"What is the crime?" asked Lamont.

"What did I say? They take life for murder only."

"My son!—a murderer!"

"They will certainly lay hands on Claude if you don't buy my silence."

"In Satan's name, who are you?"

"The man who knows!"

In the drawer before the millionaire lay a self-cocking revolver, and this flashed through his mind as he resolved upon desperate action.

"All right," he said, as nonchalantly as possible, and in a second he had opened the drawer.

The man near by stood in such a position that he could not look into the place, and he did not see Lamont's hand close about the black ivory stock of the weapon.

Suddenly the millionaire's hand leaped from the drawer and the revolver flashed in the stranger's face.

"I won't be blackmailed," hissed Lamont. "I'm as merciless as a tiger when aroused, and I count your life as nothing as compared to the welfare of my family. What is the lie you have made up for to-night's work? What is the infamous story you have planned about my son? Tell me or I will kill you where you stand, and the world will lose your infamy in this house."

The man on the carpet seemed to increase an inch in stature as he looked down into the tensely drawn face of the man of many fortunes.

"You'd do that, would you?"

"As I live I will!"

"You're a fool, Perry Lamont."

"Why so?"

"You might slay me here, but the net would be played out or drawn in all the same. You don't suppose I would place myself in your power the sole custodian of this secret which, if let out, will send your son to the electric chair? I'm no fool."

The tightly clutched weapon seemed about to fall from Lamont's hand.

"The secret is unloosed the moment I die at your hands," continued the cool stranger. "Come, treat me white, and I'll treat you the same. I want ten thousand for what I know. It saves your boy and rescues your house from disgrace."

A singular cry welled from the millionaire's throat, the revolver slipped to the floor and he sank back in the chair in a dead faint.

The stranger leaned forward and opened the drawer, and seeing something there he transferred it to an inner pocket.

CHAPTER XVII.
BACK TO THE RED SPOT.

When Carter and Mulberry Billy reached the street at the foot of Carter's stairs the boy pointed toward a cab just driving away.

"He must be in that," said Billy. "I saw him talking to a man from the cab window just now——"

"The man whose face you saw at the window of Mother Flintstone's den, Billy?"

"The same bloke."

The detective looked after the cab as it rounded a corner and then turned again to the boy.

"But the man who was spoken to from the cab?" queried the detective.

"He's gone, too."

In another instant there stepped from a doorway a few steps distant a man at whom the boy pointed excitedly.

"That's him, Mr. Carter!" he exclaimed, as the man thus singled out coolly lit a cigar.

Carter eyed him for a moment and then looked away.

The fellow walked off and the boy of the street watched him with much curiosity.

"Could you keep him in sight for me, Billy?" asked the detective.

"Just as if I'd lose him on purpose!"

Billy hurried away and watched the smoker with all the keenness he could bring to bear upon the matter.

For some time the boy was led a merry chase, for the man at first seemed to suspect that he was watched, but at last he appeared to think that he had baffled the young shadower, for he became bold and sauntered along at his ease.

Billy saw him walk up the steps of a noted clubhouse, and then stepped back to wait for his reappearance.

For this purpose the boy stationed himself in a doorway near at hand.

An hour passed, and while many came out of the club this particular one did not, and the street Arab grew a little impatient.

"Seems to me he's going ter roost there," said Billy to himself. "I'm booked for this doorway all night if he does, for I intend to keep my agreement with Mr. Carter—to watch that man till doomsday."

All at once there sounded above the boy footsteps on the stairs, and as he looked around he was pounced upon eaglelike by a hand that seemed to sink into his bones.

"Ouch!" cried the boy, as he drew back.

"Not a chirp, you young imp," hissed a voice, as he was pulled up over the steps.

Billy, of Mulberry Street, was dragged up the stairs and down a long corridor, after which he was pulled into a room by his tormentor. He heard the door locked behind him, and then the gas was quickly turned on. Then he was jammed roughly into a chair, after which he got a look at the man who had caught him.

It was not the man he had watched, but quite another person, and Billy wondered why he had caught him.

"Spying, weren't you?" said the man coolly.

"Who are you?" demanded Billy. "And don't you know you've no right to treat me this way?"

"I haven't, eh? Just wait till I'm through with you before you crow that way."

Then the man came forward and bent over Billy, who shrank into the depths of the chair.

"Who sent you after me?" he demanded.

"No one."

"No falsehood! He did, didn't he?"

"Whom do you mean?"

"You know."

"You must explain."

"Just as if you didn't know anything, you little gutter rat! To be plain, the man you were talking to to-night told you to dog my steps. I know that much."

"Then that keeps me from explainin'," smiled Billy, whereat the man's face grew dark.

"No insolence! Little chicks get their necks wrung same as old ones."

Billy leaped from the chair and sprang forward, but he was arrested by the hand of the fellow and held fast.

"Tell me the truth. He sent you after me?"

For once in his life at least Mulberry Billy was terrified.

"Yes," he said.

"Nick Carter they call him, don't they?"

"Yes."

"Detective!"

The boy said nothing.

"Why am I to be watched?"

"I don't know."

"What has happened lately?"

"Don't you know? Don't you ever read the papers?"

"Sometimes."

"Then you must know that they've killed Mother Flintstone."

"Who's she?"

"My best friend, even if she didn't have all the frills of society," said Billy, with a grin.

"Where did she live?"

"In Hell's Kitchen."

"That's a nice name!"

"It fits the place."

"What was Mother Flintstone?"

"She fenced some times."

"Oho!" The exclamation was followed by a prolonged whistle. "I see."

The man, dropping Billy suddenly, took several turns about the room.

"Could you show me where she lived, boy?" he suddenly asked, coming back to the boy.

"I could——"

"And you will? That's good! Mother Flintstone, eh? Was that her right name?"

"Never heard any other for the old woman."

The countenance of the stranger seemed to soften and he told the boy to guide him.

They left the house together, the boy in advance, and Billy piloted the man into Mulberry Bend and straight to Hell's Kitchen.

"It's a tough place, I see," was all the comment the stranger made as they entered the locality.

"No place tougher, but I've called it home for a long time."

Into the little old room—the place of sin and crime—Billy led the man and a light was struck.

"Where did she keep her valuables?" asked the man.

"I don't know."

"But she had papers, hadn't she?"

"I can't say; but if she had the perlice must have found them."

"They searched the den, eh?"

"They looked it over."

"Did Carter do it, too?"

"Yes."

"What did he find?"

The boy shook his head.

"You're not the custodian of his secrets, I see."

"I'm not."

"Let me see what I can find."

The man began to go through the place, watched by the boy with all eyes. He was a good-looking fellow, only his beard seemed a little too black and glossy to be natural, and the boy had an idea that it had never grown on his face.

All at once the man turned and looked at Billy.

At the same time he put out one hand, and it fell upon a dusty shelf on one side of the room.

"Turn your back a moment, boy," he commanded.

Billy did so, and while he looked away he was certain that the stranger did something.

When again he looked around the man was standing at his ease and his face was as calm as ever.

"Look yonder," suddenly cried the boy, pointing at the window. "There it is again."

The stranger turned in an instant, and then looked at the street Arab.

"I see nothing at the window," he said.

"It's gone now. That's the second time I saw it there."

"A face, was it, boy?"

"Yes; the face of the man who killed Mother Flintstone!"

"Then it's not far off."

With this the stranger ran out of the place, and Billy heard him in the narrow court beyond.

"In the name of Satan, who is he?" ejaculated the boy, while he waited for the man's return.

His question was followed by a sharp report, and in a second the boy was outside.

He smelled powder the moment he opened the door, and then a human figure fell at his feet.

Billy sprang back with a cry and heard a half-suppressed oath and flying footsteps.

"Say, boy," said a voice, as the little fellow stooped over a prostrate man on the bricks.

"Did you see him?"

"Only a glimpse."

"Well, he's got me—just as I expected. But he didn't get the documents."

"What documents?"

"Mother Flintstone's. They're here."

The wounded speaker laid one hand on his left breast. He tried to rise, but sank again to the stones, and Billy could only look on, white-faced and breathless.

"You want a doctor and the perlice," he said at last.

"Neither one," growled the man through set teeth. "I don't want them, I say. I'm not dead yet, though they gave me a close call to-night. Help me up. There, you see I can stand all right. I feel better already. I'm worth ten dead men, and in an hour I'll be worth fifty. Come, let us get out of this."

Billy was not loath to go, and they glided from the scene and struck the street in a few seconds.

"Great Cæsar!" cried the boy, falling back from the man the moment he got a glimpse of him in the lamplight. "Be you the devil or Tom Walker——"

The man stopped the boy by throwing his hand to his face.

The black beard was gone and the skin was smooth, and this was what had called forth the street urchin's exclamation.

CHAPTER XVIII.
THE FATE OF A SPY.

Under the ground at last Mother Flintstone passed from the minds of many. The hovel she had occupied in Hell's Kitchen got other tenants and the crime was forgotten.

Not by everybody, however, for in the mind of more than one person the old woman whose life no one seemed to know beyond a few years was of some importance.

Carter was on the trail, and he was destined to find it one of the strangest if not the most exciting of his varied career. Nick had just learned that Brockey Gann had been sent to Sing Sing for a short term, and that Mrs. Lawrence and her daughter had gone abroad, never to return to this country.

It was the night after his last adventure—the one on the street with Billy, of Mulberry Street—when the boy failed to point out the man he had seen, that he stood in another part of the city.

The famous detective was quite alone, and his gaze was riveted upon a man who stood in front of a swell café lighting a cigar.

This person was well dressed and looked as if he belonged to uppertendom.

His features were regular, though they showed some signs of fashionable dissipation, and he carried a cane with an elaborate gold head.

In short, this person was Claude Lamont, the son of the millionaire, who had lately received the man who wanted ten thousand dollars to keep a secret.

Lamont was a favorite at the club because he spent his father's money freely, and at times gave swell suppers, which were the talk of the town.

Young Lamont appeared to be waiting for some one, and presently that individual came out of the café. He looked a good deal like Claude, only he seemed to be several years his junior, and when the two met they walked away together.

Carter followed.

The men were talking earnestly, and at last Carter heard Lamont say:

"You didn't make it with the governor, eh?"

"No; confound it all. He fainted just when I thought I had landed the fish, and I came away with an empty hook."

"That's bad."

"Couldn't have been worse."

"Shall I try again?"

"No, we must take another tack," and then Claude laughed.

This was all the detective heard, and the pair walked a little faster.

After a while Carter let them go and turned his attention to another part of the town.

This time he pushed his way into an upper room in one of the most disreputable localities and confronted a man who nearly leaped from a chair at sight of him.

"Never mind. Don't get excited, Jack," smiled the detective. "I'm not after you this time."

The fellow, who was past thirty, with a slim face covered with a beard of a week's growth, seemed pleased, but at the same time he snarled like a wild beast.

"I've got work for you," said the detective.

"Not for me, no, sir! I won't do any man's work—not even yours," he growled.

"Come, Jack. It won't get you into trouble."

"I won't, there!"

The speaker settled back into his chair and looked ugly.

"You remember Mother Flintstone?"

"Yes, and I know she's dead."

"And buried."

"I hope so, but I don't care what they've done with her. I am out of the business."

"You know Claude Lamont?"

"The money king's son? Of course I do, and I know nothing very good of him, either."

"Well, Jack, I want you to get on with him."

"I say no."

The voice was determined, but this fact did not check the detective.

"Listen to me, Jack."

"Not if you want to make a sleuth out of me."

"I don't—in a sense."

"But you want me to get in with this young lion and get the worst of the bargain."

Carter thought a moment.

Was there not some other way of bringing this man to time?

Nick had befriended him once, had saved him from a term up the river; and now he needed him.

Jack Redmond was a clever, all-around crook, and, at the same time, he knew how to spy and do anything that required wits and cunning.

Suddenly Nick turned again to the man and said:

"You know Margie?"

At this Redmond started and seemed to shiver.

"Where is she?" he eagerly inquired.

"Where she can be found at any time."

"Do you know?"

"Will you help me?"

Redmond sprang up and confronted the detective with a quick look.

"Does she think of me yet?"

"I can't say that."

"Will you help me with Margie?"

"So far as I can."

"Then I'm yours!"

For a moment the detective watched the man and held out his hand; but the crook refused it.

"No, I'm yours. You've bought me," he said. "Now, what am I to do?"

For some time the detective talked, and was not interrupted.

When he went away he seemed to smile to himself, and half an hour later he was back in his own rooms.

One hour later Claude Lamont was met in the club annex by a man, who held out his hand.

Lamont looked searchingly at this person and shook his head.

"You have the best of me," said he.

"What, don't you know me?" cried the other, as if surprised. "I'm Belmont."

"The devil you are!"

"That's who I am, and I'm not surprised that you did not recognize me."

"I thought you were dead—in fact, three years ago I read about your death at sea."

"So did thousands," laughed the so-called Belmont, who was Jack Redmond, the crook. "I thought at one time I was on the brink of eternity. We had nine tough weeks on a tropical island, but were saved by a liner."

This seemed to satisfy Lamont, for he fell to talking to Redmond, and the two adjourned to the wine-room and opened several bottles.

It was midnight before they parted, and then Redmond slunk away.

He had broken the ice.

"To-morrow," said he, "I will go a little further, and before the week's out I'll have my clutches on this man for Carter. He doesn't suspect, and I've completely hoodwinked him."

Jack went back to his little den, but did not lock the door.

Ten minutes later he heard footsteps on the stair, and, thinking that Carter was coming back, he watched the door with some curiosity.

When the door opened he got pale, for instead of the detective another man stood before him.

"Spy and informer, your time has come!" cried this person, who seemed as wiry as a tiger as he crossed the room.

Jack Redmond started from his chair, but a revolver was thrust into his face, and he fell back.

"Silence! Not a word! That was a cool game you played to-night," continued the other.

"What game?" stammered the crook.

"You know, and it's going to cost you your treacherous life."

"No."

"Yes, I say—your life!"

Jack looked into the muzzle of the weapon and wondered if he could cross the space between them and seize the man before he could press the trigger.

"You told a plausible tale, and he believed you. You passed yourself off as Belmont, who lies in fifty fathoms of water, and he took it all for gospel. You've got to die."

The crook said nothing.

"Sit down," commanded the stranger.

Involuntarily Jack sat down and awaited the fellow's next movement.

"What have you to say before you die? Any word to send to any person?"

"You don't mean to take my life?"

"I do. It isn't worth the snuffing of a candle just now. All the money in the world could not save you."

Suddenly Jack was pounced upon by the human wolf and crushed deeper into the chair.

A pair of demon hands seemed to meet behind his windpipe, and he tried, but vainly, to rise.

His eyes bulged from his head, his tongue protruded and he emitted a groan.

Three minutes later the demon arose and looked down at the dark face in the chair.

Then he went through the crook's pockets and found nothing of value even to him.

Behind Jack was a wall tolerably white, and the murderer went toward it. He took a pencil from his pocket and wrote in scrawling characters across the surface a few words that seemed to please him.

"That's it. He'll see it," he hissed. "And he'll know that it is a death trail if he persists."

In another moment the little den was tenanted by no one but the silent man in the chair.

The gas burned over his head, sicklylike and blue, and the room seemed filled with a noxious odor.

It burned on till the first streaks of morning revealed the city, and pedestrians reappeared on the sidewalks.

No one came.

Several hours passed and the streets swarmed again with their eager thousands.

Then the door was opened and Carter came in.

He stood stock-still at sight of the dead man—his spy—in the chair, and then he happened to glance at the wall.

In another second he was there, and his bulging eyes had read:

"The spy first, the master next! There is no escape for him!"

CHAPTER XIX.
THE KNOCK-OUT DROPS.

The man of many trails read the inscription on the wall more than once before he turned away.

It meant him.

There was not the least doubt of this, and for some time the detective stood rooted to the spot, as it were, and looked at what appeared to be a record of doom.

At last he went over to the dead man in the chair, and, lifting the body, he knew what had terminated Jack Redmond's career.

The hands of some fiend had strangled him, and Nick seemed to inspect the marks on the throat for the time that had elapsed since the tragedy.

Slowly and with deliberation the detective quitted the scene of crime and went down the steps.

At the bottom he nearly ran against a woman with a black shawl pulled over her head in such a manner as to conceal her features. She tried to escape the detective, but the detective's hand shot out and drew her toward him.

With the other hand he removed the shawl and looked into a wan face seamed with want and dissipation.

"You know Jack?" he said.

"Heavens! Jack! Yes."

"Will you go up and see him?"

She fell back, but the hand stayed her.

"He did it, then?" she cried.

"You saw some one, then?"

"Yes; but for Heaven's sake don't mix me up in anything like murder."

Carter watched the nervous twitching of the woman's lips and waited for her to calm herself.

"When was he here?" he asked.

"Last night."

"What was he like?"

"He was rather tall, and had a step as stealthy as a tiger's."

"You saw him come?"

"Yes."

"And go?"

"I did."

"How long was the man upstairs?"

"Not over twenty minutes."

"Did you suspect a crime?"

"I did; but I hadn't the nerve to go up after he went away. I only guessed his mission."

Nick at last released the creature, who had in the meantime called herself Gutter Nan for identification, and went away.

"It's the second crime," was all the remark he made to himself.

The detective sent word to police headquarters, and as the crime, like the murder of Mother Flintstone, came too late for the morning papers, the afternoon journals got it.

No one knew among the reporters that Jack Redmond had been Carter's spy.

None was told who was meant by "the master" in the sentence on the wall; they only guessed at that, and some queer guesses they made, too.

Carter found Margie Marne that same day, and the girl's first question was about his trail.

"I've got a strange letter here," said the girl, handing the detective a note she had just received.

The detective drew it from the envelope and read as follows:

"MISS MARNE: If you want to hear of something to your advantage please come to the Trocadero to-day at two and enter the first stall on the right. Come alone, for this is business of importance, and greatly concerns you.

"BUSINESS."

After reading the message the detective looked up and found the eyes of the girl riveted upon his face.

"Well?" he asked.

"Shall I go?"

"Yes."

"I'll do anything you tell me to," was the reply, and a faint smile flitted across the girl's face.

"Have you fears, Margie?"

"Yes. I fear all the time ever since the death of Mother Flintstone."

"Who, think you, is 'Business'?"

"An enemy."

"Then, why go to the Trocadero?"

"Because you say so."

Carter promised the girl that he would not be far off at the hour mentioned in the letter, and Margie agreed to be on hand. He did not see fit to tell her about Jack Redmond's death, as it might unnerve her, and, bidding her good-by, he left the house.

It was near two that afternoon when a man, who would not have been taken for Nick, entered the Trocadero on the Bowery, and seating himself at a table called for a drink.

The place was not very well filled at the time, and while he sipped his wine the detective looked around the place.

Presently he saw a man enter and go straight to the stall designated by the letter to Margie, and the door was closed behind him.

Now Carter began to wait for the girl, and ten minutes later she came in.

Glancing up and down the place as if looking for him Carter saw her enter the same stall and heard a slight ejaculation when she found it occupied.

Just then the detective moved his seat to a table nearer the stall and indulged again.

After drinking a third glass a strange feeling of drowsiness seemed to take possession of him, and he tried to shake it off.

In vain, however, did he battle against the feeling, it only grew stronger, till at last he became aware that he was sinking into unconsciousness.

His last recollection was of trying to rise and then sinking down upon the chair, while everything became black about him.

When the detective came to, a singular feeling racked his head and he felt dizzy.

With some effort he managed to stagger to his feet and then he went to the suspected stall.

The door now stood slightly ajar, and he pushed it open, but the place was empty.

Where was Margie, and what had taken place in that secluded spot where perhaps more than one crime had been committed?

After looking at the table and taking in the whole stall the detective shut the door and started toward the walk.

He knew the fame of the Trocadero.

More than once a trail had led him across its precincts, and on several occasions he had picked up important clews under its roof.

But now he himself was the victim of trickery, the dupe of crime, for he doubted not that the drinks had been drugged by some infamous hand and for a purpose.

Behind the bar stood the man who had carried the drinks to him, a little man with one of the worst faces, and the detective thought he looked at him with wonderment as if surprised that he—Carter—had escaped death.

Fixing his eyes upon this man he leaned over the bar and said:

"What became of the girl?"

The little wretch only grinned and turned away to wait on a new customer.

But he was not to get rid of the champion detective so easily, for the hand of Carter darted over the counter and fastened on him like the talons of a vulture.

In Nick's grip the man was a babe, and as the hand seemed to sink to his bones he emitted a whimper that sounded like a whine and looked blankly into the detective's face.

"I—I never saw the girl," he cried.

"No lies, sir. I want the truth. Who told you to drug me?"

"No one. I—I drug nobody. I'm honest."

"So is Satan," hissed the detective, and just then the little wretch appealed to the owner of the establishment for protection.

"No interference, Number Six," said the detective, with a look at the broad-shouldered owner of the Trocadero, and the man thus designated winced.

"Tell the gentleman the truth, Caddy," he said to the little man; but that person was still stubborn.

"Caddy" hoped to be released without being forced to tell the truth, but the detective had no idea of doing this.

He actually pulled Caddy over the counter, to the amusement of the few people in the place at the time, and, putting his ear close to the barkeeper's, he said:

"The truth or Sing Sing. Take your choice!"

This seemed to have a wonderful effect at once.

The detective escorted Caddy down the sawdusted aisle and pushed him into the first stall.

"Where did they go?" he asked.

Caddy was very meek now, and his voice trembled as he spoke.

"They went out the back entrance," he said.

"Both of them?"

"Yes."

"How was the girl?"

"I don't know."

"Did she seem to go willingly with the man?"

"I don't think she did."

"Was there a cab in the alley out there?"

"Yes."

For a moment Carter looked daggers at the little scoundrel, his indignation fast rising, but he kept his temper as he said:

"You were that man's agent. You fixed my drinks at his suggestion or command."

"He paid me for it."

"But how did he designate me?"

"He told me to fix the gentleman at a certain table—that's all I know."

"Look here! You've played a cool hand for a great villain, and if anything happens to the girl I'll hold you, in part, responsible. Who was the man?"

"I don't know."

"You do know," cried Carter, and again his hand fell upon Caddy's shoulder. "You didn't do all this for a total stranger. They don't do such things in the Trocadero. You know that man! Now who was he?"

The little man could not avoid the sharp eyes of the best detective in New York, and he felt the hand on his shoulder grow more viselike as the question was put.

"Tell me. That or Sing Sing!" said Carter.

"He's a rich bloke's son," answered Caddy.

"That's not enough. Who is he? You know!"

"They call him Claude Lamont."

CHAPTER XX.
AN INCORRUPTIBLE DETECTIVE.

"Ha, ha," laughed Nick to himself. "So Mr. Lamont is playing a nice little hand. We'll see about it," and then he turned his attention again to the man he had in tow.

"He told you to dose me, did he?"

Caddy nodded.

"Did he say why?"

"No."

"But he was anxious to have me drugged?"

"He seemed so."

"Now, don't you know where he took the girl?"

The little barkeeper of the Trocadero shook his head in a solemn manner, and Carter felt that he was in earnest.

"He hasn't been back since?" he asked.

"No."

The detective went to the back entrance of the place and saw where a cab had stood.

Beyond doubt this was the vehicle in which Margie Marne had disappeared with Claude Lamont, and after looking the ground over without finding an additional clew, Carter went back.

It might be hard to track the cab, as there were hundreds in the city, and under the influence of Claude's money the drivers would not like to betray a good customer.

The detective put this and that together, and in a short time he might have been seen on the front steps of the Lamont mansion.

It was his first visit to the place, and he did not disguise himself in the least.

It was not a very fashionable hour for a call, but his ring caused the door to open and he was ushered in by a wondering maid.

"Is Mr. Lamont in?" asked the detective.

"Yes, sir, but he is indisposed."

Sick or well, the detective had come to see the millionaire, and he was not to be cheated out of his game.

Handing the servant his card he waited in the hall, and presently she came back asking him to step into the library.

This the detective did, and in a few moments he stood face to face with Lamont.

He had seen the nabob on several occasions, but he seemed to have greatly aged in a short time and his face looked haggard and pale.

Lamont looked up at his visitor and tried to place him, but failed.

"I don't know you," said he, glancing down at the detective's card, which he held in his hand.

Carter, who had taken a chair opposite the man, said in his peculiar tones:

"I am a detective. I have come here on a matter of business which may concern you."

"I am at a loss to know how."

"In the first place, sir, are we alone?"

"Entirely so."

The detective, in spite of this assurance, lowered his voice.

"Whatever became of your sister, Mr. Lamont?"

There was a quick start, and the face of the millionaire got white.

"I never had a sister," said he, with an effort.

"Make sure of that. Whatever became of her, I ask?"

Lamont looked around the room like a wild beast seeking a loophole of escape, but seeing none he came back to the detective.

"Pardon me for trying to deceive you," said he. "That is the black spot on our family history. I had a sister once. But she is dead now."

"Her name was———"

"Hester."

"And you say she is dead?"

"She is."

"When did her death take place?"

"Some twenty years ago."

A faint smile came to the detective's face, and for half a second he looked searchingly into Lamont's.

"Why try to deceive me?" he said. "You know that this sister died within the last few days."

"What's that?" and the millionaire almost started from his chair, while his hands clutched the sides of it like a madman.

"She died by violence," coolly continued the detective. "She was murdered—not for her money, for she hadn't much. But she was killed all the same."

"I can't believe that," cried Lamont.

"Nevertheless it is true. Mother Flintstone was your sister, Mr. Lamont."

"That old hag? Impossible!"

"It is the truth, and, what is more, you knew it."

"It is false!"

"Shall I prove it?" asked the detective, not in the least abating his coolness. "Shall I prove beyond cavil to you that Mother Flintstone was your sister?"

"Who are you, man or devil?" exclaimed the money king. "And what can buy your silence?"

"I have told you who I am, and nothing on earth can buy my silence."

"You don't want to disgrace my family?"

"I am serving justice just now, no matter who is disgraced."

"It will kill my wife and daughter."

"Even that event will not take me from my trail."

"You have no heart."

"Neither had the man who killed that old woman."

"Who did it? Tell me that!"

"I am not quite prepared to answer, but in time I will be. I am here to tell you that the death of your ostracized sister shall be avenged, no matter whose neck the rope stretches, figuratively speaking."

"You don't mean to insinuate that I had a hand in the crime?"

"I make no charges. I merely called to ask if she was not your sister?"

"I've answered that question."

"And you let her go to the potter's field?"

"I did, and I would do it again under the circumstances."

"Don't talk to me about my having no heart, Mr. Lamont."

"I couldn't think of acknowledging her and having the body in my house."

"That's all."

Nick arose and was watched by the man with a look like that of a tiger.

Perry Lamont seemed to bite his lips through and his eyes emitted sparks of rage.

As the detective stepped toward the door it opened and a tall and distinguished-looking young lady entered the room.

"My daughter," said the millionaire, with a wave of his hand toward the young lady, but she did not seem to hear the words.

Already she had turned upon Carter and her hands were clenched till the nails seemed to cut the fair flesh to the palms.

"You want to disgrace us all!" she cried, as she appeared to increase an inch in stature. "You are one of those blackmailers with whom honest and wealthy people must be bothered. You want to make us trouble. But you shall not! Father shall not pay you one dollar to keep the false secret you think you have discovered. Attempt to carry out your plans and your life will not be worth the snuffing of a candle."

Carter was astounded at these words, and he could not take his eyes from the flushed face of the girl who was really beautiful and vixenish.

"Be calm, miss," said he. "I don't intend to disgrace your family name. The truth never hurt anybody. I am a detective on the trail, and if that trail leads to your house, why, you should not find fault, for the dogs of justice seldom miss the scent."

"But you just said the old creature murdered in her hovel a few nights ago was my father's sister."

"Ask him."

Carter waved his hand toward the motionless man in the chair.

"Father has not been himself for some time, and to-night is not accountable for the admissions he may have made."

Carter looked again at Perry Lamont, whose gaze had wandered to his daughter, and his hands, clasped before, had fallen apart.

At that moment he did look like a man half demented, but the detective soon returned to the tall girl.

"You shan't ruin us," she cried. "You shall not unite our name with that of Mother Flintstone, whose life, I am told, was anything but honest. It will be worth your life to do this."

The look which accompanied these words told him that they were meant for a terrible threat, and the tightly shut hands of the speaker were proof that she was a fitting sister for Claude Lamont.

"We will meet again, perhaps," said the detective. "I am going to run the guilty down. That is my present mission."

At this moment Perry Lamont raised his head and looked at the detective.

"I'm not to be trifled with," said he. "I can make it hot for the man who brings us down to Mother Flintstone's level."

"Well, you may proceed to do your worst," was the cool answer. "You may be 'disgraced,' as you say, by the relationship, but this affair must not stop there."

With this parting shot the detective put out his hand to open the door, but the white fingers of the daughter closed about his wrist.

"Beware," she almost hissed. "I don't know who took the old hag's life, but you must not connect her with our family."

The detective shook the grip off and looked again at Perry Lamont.

His head had dropped upon his breast, and his face was deathly white.

"He's gone into one of his strange spells," said the girl. "You see that he is almost an imbecile. At times he seems his old self, but in reality he is but a human wreck. I'll give you ten thousand dollars to quit this 'trail,' as you call it."

Ten thousand dollars!

Nick was silent and the girl took it as a sign of hesitation.

"I'll write out the check now," she went on. "It shall be paid any way you want it."

The detective shook his head.

"You won't, eh?" cried Miss Lamont.

"I'm simply Nick Carter, and he has never been in the market, miss," was the response.

In an instant the girl's countenance changed again from expectancy to wrath. She opened the door and pointed into the hall.

"Take what comes!" she hissed, and with this Carter walked out.

CHAPTER XXI.
THE CARD CLEW.

Jack Redmond's death promised to give the police of New York another job, but no one suspected that he was Carter's spy.

The woman who had seen the strange man go up to Redmond's room had given her information to the detective alone, and Nick kept it to himself.

He did not doubt that the crook had been put out of the way because he was on the right trail in the matter of spying, and as he—Carter—had set Jack to keep track of Claude Lamont, he resolved to turn his own attention to that young man.

Then, the disappearance of Margie from the Trocadero, whither she had gone to meet a person discovered to be the millionaire's son, was an additional incentive for the detective, and he went from Lamont's mansion to a certain part of the city where he expected to find the heir.

Through it all he did not lose sight of the fact that he was Mother Flintstone's avenger.

That he kept in mind all the time, and with all his foresight he went back to the original trail.

It was some time after the exciting interview we have just recorded as taking place in the palatial home of the retired money king that the figure of Carter might have been seen to enter one of the fashionable clubrooms of the city.

No one would have known him without an introduction, and no one did.

Attired like a person well-to-do, with sleek garments and a glossy beard over his smooth face, the detective sat down in the smoking room.

The room was most brilliantly lit up and expensively furnished, but the detective who had trailed men in every walk of life was not astonished.

He drew a cigar from his pocket and puffed leisurely away, all the time taking a good survey of the place.

A number of rich young men lounged about the room, filling the plush chairs, while on the floor above could be heard the noise of the billiard balls.

Presently a young man entered the smoking room and took a seat nearly opposite the detective.

It was Claude Lamont.

Perry Lamont's son showed signs of high living, for his face was florid and his nerves a little unstrung. He was faultlessly attired, for he had the best tailor money could procure, and the detective watched him furtively while he appeared to enjoy his Havana.

Claude Lamont seemed to have a good deal of time on his hands, and so did Carter.

All at once a messenger boy entered the smoking room and looked around.

Spying Claude, he hastened to him and handed him a letter.

"Ha!" thought the watchful detective. "He is not forgotten to-night, and now we'll see if it is an important message."

Claude tipped the boy and opened the letter. He started a little as his eye fell upon the page and quickly glanced up as if to see if he were watched.

Then he settled down to a quiet perusal of the message, during which time Carter got a good look at the workings of his countenance.

"Hang it all. It comes just when I don't want to be bothered with the matter," growled Claude, as he rammed the message hurriedly into his pocket and then went toward the cloakroom.

Carter watched him through the open door and saw the letter drop from his pocket as he put on his overcoat.

Lamont walked out without noticing his loss, and the moment he vanished, the letter was in the detective's hands.

In another second Nick vanished, too, and as he came out upon the steps in front of the club he spied Lamont flitting around the nearest corner.

"Let him go. The quarry will not be missed just yet," smiled the detective, and then he went into a near café and in one of the private stalls opened the letter.

"Didn't want this matter to come up just now," he laughed, as he glanced down the page. "Well, I should think not."

It did not take the man of many trails long to master the lost missive, and when he finished he read what follows:

"Mr. Claude Lamont: I send you this for the last time. I will not be put off another day, and you must take the consequences, if you have the hardihood to do it. You know what I know, and if you do not come down I will unseal my lips. You fly high, like a bird with golden plumage, but I'll clip your feathers and bring you to prison if you don't pay attention to this letter. When my lips are unsealed there'll be the biggest sensation New York has ever had, and you know it. Don't put me off another day. You know what this means. I'm master of the field, and I can wreck your every hope and blight your fashionable life.

"IMOGENE."

Twice did the detective read this over, and every word seemed to engrave itself upon his mind.

Quietly he folded the letter and smiled.

Who was "Imogene"?

Looking for her would be like hunting for a needle in the gutters of Gotham.

That she was a desperate woman the letter told him, and he did not wonder that it paled Claude Lamont's cheeks.

Perhaps if he had followed the young man he might have been guided by him to Imogene's home, but he had to be content for the present with the letter.

Nick, with the letter reposing in an inner pocket, came out of the café and for a moment stood under the lights that revealed the sidewalk.

"I'll find the boy now," he said. "Billy may have discovered something since I last saw him."

Ten minutes later he entered a little room on Mulberry Street and aroused a boy who was sleeping on a rude couch.

It was not far from Mother Flintstone's late hovel, and Billy looked astonished to see the detective in the den.

"Been dreamin' erbout you, Mr. Carter," cried the boy, as he rubbed his eyes.

"Well, I'll listen to the dream, Billy."

"No, it wasn't any good, but all the time I saw your face in it. You know the man who dragged me from Mother Flintstone's?"

"Yes."

"I ran afoul of him to-night."

"Where, Billy?"

"Back in the old place, but this time he didn't get to handle me."

"No?"

"See here. He lost this in the house. It fell from his pocket when he pulled his handkerchief out," and Billy handed the detective a card.

"Did you follow him after he left the old house?" he asked the boy.

"No. I just let him go, for I wanted to see what was on this card, for you, Mr. Carter."

"Thanks, Billy."

The name on the card stood out in bold relief to Nick's gaze, and he saw there one he might have seen before.

"You don't know this George Richmond, do you, Billy?" he asked, looking down at the boy on the edge of the bed.

"I don't."

"George Richmond is a well-known man in certain quarters, but of late he hasn't shown up often."

"Is he crooked, Mr. Carter?"

"Yes, in a manner. How did he look to-night, Billy?"

"He wore a brown beard and was well dressed."

"Did he limp a little?"

"Bless me if he didn't, but I wouldn't have thought of that if you hadn't mentioned it."

The detective seemed satisfied.

"What did he seem to want in Mother Flintstone's old quarters?"

"I hardly know. He sounded several of the walls, as if looking for a secret door, but he didn't appear to find one."

"Anything else?"

"He went over the floor like a fox, with his nose close to the boards."

"Was that all?"

"No, he even sounded the ceiling."

"Quite particular," smiled the detective.

"Wasn't he, though? I never saw anything just like that. He didn't let an inch of space escape him."

"Did he seem excited?"

"Not a bit of it. He was as cool as a cucumber, and not for a minute did he get off his base. He seemed disappointed, though, that's all—as if he expected to find some hidden wealth and didn't, you see."

"Maybe he overlooked it, Billy."

"I don't think there was any to overlook," said the boy. "But, really, there's no telling what that man was huntin', but he wasn't thar for any good you can bet your neck, Mr. Carter."

"I'll agree with you on that score, boy," and the detective put the card in his pocket. "George Richmond never goes out after small game. That's his record."

"Do you think he had anything to do with the murder of Mother Flintstone?" eagerly questioned the boy.

"Time will tell," was the detective's reply. "Do you think he had, Billy?"

"I do, I do," cried the boy. "Bless me if I kin get the idea out o' my head. That man either killed Mother Flintstone or he knows who did."

To this the detective made no reply, and he told the boy to go back to bed.

"Have you struck any clew yet, Mr. Carter?" asked Billy.

"A little one. There, go to bed and let me go to work again."

"I will, but keep an eye on the man I saw to-night in Mother Flintstone's house. He needs watchin' day and night. Good night, Mr. Carter."

Five minutes later the famous detective was far from Billy's uncouth abode, and in an entirely different part of the city.

He stopped at last, and looked up at a tall building that seemed to cleave the darkened sky far overhead.

The brief inspection seemed to satisfy him, for he entered the main hallway and began to climb the uncarpeted stair.

He reached the third floor before he encountered any one, and there he was suddenly brought to a halt by a voice that rang down the ghostly corridor.

"Another step on your life! I have you at my mercy and I never fail to bring down my man. Stand where you are, for another step means a bullet in your brain!"

CHAPTER XXII.
THE BIRD IN THE DEATH TRAP.

Leaving Carter, the shadow, in the net of doom, let us go back a little in our story of crime and see how fared one of our other characters.

You will recollect Margie Marne's visit to the Trocadero in answer to the mysterious note which had reached her, and how the detective discovered that the person whom she encountered vanished with her into the alley back of the café while the detective himself was coolly and cleverly drugged by Caddy.

If the detective could have tracked the cab he would have seen it stop in front of a frame building not far from the East River.

He would have seen the door open and a man step out.

This person looked cautiously around, as if he feared he had been followed, but seeing that no one was on his track, he reached into the dark depths of the vehicle and brought out a limp form.

It was the form of the young girl, and he hastily carried her into the house.

Margie looked unconscious, as, indeed, she was, for she made no move of any kind, and once in the old house the man laid his burden on a sofa.

Then he went outside and spoke to the man on the box of the cab and the vehicle rattled away.

All this did not occupy much time, and had been accomplished as neatly as ever a dastardly job was.

Soon afterward there was a slight movement on the part of the girl on the sofa, and Margie looked up.

She seemed to have an indistinct recollection of what had taken place, for she arose with difficulty and tottered across the darkened apartment.

"This is not home," she exclaimed. "Neither is it the café where I met the stranger. What has happened and how came I to this house? I will not remain here. I must get out of this trap, for trap it must surely be."

She found the door, but could not open it, and then, as a full sense of the horror overtook her, she fell to the floor.

The next second the door opened softly, and a man looked into the room.

His face, which was rather handsome, was full of devilish triumph, and for half a second he gloated over the body on the carpet.

"Caught," he said. "Caught like a fly in the spider's web! You didn't give us much trouble, girl. We expected a little more than we met. But it's all right. Now the coast will soon be clear. I'll just turn you over to Nora."

He went away with the last word on his lips, and five minutes later a woman entered the room. She looked like a typical jaileress, for she was tall, lean, rawboned and dark-faced.

She smiled when she saw Margie.

"Another one!" she grinned. "This one won't give me much trouble. Why, she's but a girl. And such hands, too! I wonder where he netted her?"

She went to work restoring Margie to consciousness, and in a short time succeeded.

At sight of her the young girl put forth her hands in pleading gesture, but when the light fell upon the woman's face she shuddered and turned away.

"That's right. I'm no beauty," said the woman. "I'm no princess like the one in the fairy tale. They call me Nora, if you want to get acquainted with me. Call me Nora, nothing more."

"But you've got another name?"

"Guess not! Nora's good enough for me."

"Then Nora, where am I?"

"In my house."

"Who brought me here?"

"There, don't ask too many questions," smiled the dark jaileress. "You are liable to get some lies if you do."

"What, are you in the plot, too?"

"I know my business," evasively answered the woman. "You don't think I live here for nothing, little one?"

Margie felt hope almost desert her soul.

"But you don't intend to keep me here," she cried. "You have no right to do that."

"I obey orders, never asking any questions."

"Then it is a plot against me. I remember the visit to the café. It was a decoy letter, after all. I went; I fell into the snare and here I am—lost!"

"Don't take such a black view of matters and things," was the reply. "Mebbe they aren't quite as dark as you paint them."

"They are dark enough," said the despairing girl. "You shall not keep me here."

"Very well. Then go."

Margie bounded across the room and caught the doorknob wildly.

"Why don't you open the door?" coolly asked Nora.

"Heavens, I cannot!"

"That's the easiest way to find out. No, you can't get out till I say so."

Margie looked at the woman and then once more at the window between her and the street.

"I'll call for help," she exclaimed.

"All right, miss."

In a moment the poor girl was at the window, but when she drew back the curtain she saw inner shutters of iron.

Truly she was in durance.

"Why am I here? Surely you will tell me that? What have I done to deserve this fate?"

"Wait and see. You want some sleep, don't you?"

"In this terrible house? No!"

"But you must take a little rest. Come."

Nora gripped Margie's wrist and led her from the room. She escorted her upstairs and into a smaller apartment on the floor, where she pointed toward a bed.

"Not a particle of sleep till you tell me why I am treated thus," cried the distracted girl.

"Then you'll remain a long while awake," was the quick answer. "I'll tell you nothing."

Margie grew desperate. She darted forward and clutched the woman's sleeve and looking into her face saw it grow white.

"Tell me!" cried Margie. "I am the victim of some awful plot. Is it because I am the detective's friend?"

"The detective?" echoed Nora. "What detective?"

"Nicholas Carter."

The name had a magical effect on the woman, for she shrank as far away as Margie's hand would let her, and for half a minute gazed into the girl's face.

"Where is he?" she cried.

"On the trail."

"On what trail?"

"On the trail of the hand that stilled Mother Flintstone's life."

"My God! Can this be true, girl?"

"It is true, and because I am Nick's friend I am here. You know him."

Nora did not speak, but her lips parted in a gasp and she looked away.

"You don't want that man to implicate you in the plot, do you?" asked Margie.

No answer.

"You don't want to hang with the balance?"

"I won't; the rope that hangs me isn't made. The hemp has never grown for that purpose."

"Then let me out of here."

"To tell on me—to go to Carter with the story of where you've been?"

"I'll shield you, Nora."

Margie thought she was making headway with her jaileress, but the next moment dispelled her hopes.

"Not for the world, girl," said Nora. "I can't afford to do that. It would doom me."

"But this man will find out. He intends to discover the hand that took the old woman's life. The murderer never escapes Nick Carter. He is doomed from the moment the trail is found."

"I know him."

"Then you don't want to be dragged into his net. I am more than Margie Marne. I have another name, as I verily believe, and the man who brought me here knows that."

"I cannot say."

"It is the foulest plot ever hatched in this or any other city. Look here: Mother Flintstone lived alone in squalor and apparent poverty. One night she is killed—stabbed in the neck. Why was the life of the old woman taken?

Who was the man who came back to the window, back to the scene of his crime to be discovered by little Billy, the street rat? What was Mother Flintstone to that man?"

"Was he the murderer?" asked Nora.

"If not, why did he come there? As I live, I believe that man has Mother Flintstone's blood on his hands."

"I don't know," she said, dropping her voice almost to a whisper. "But go to sleep, girl. I can't let you out."

In another moment Margie was alone, for the woman had broken from her grasp, and the girl heard her footsteps on the stairs beyond the room.

"I see. This woman is merely the tool of the plotters," thought the detective's fair friend. "She serves them, while she fears Mr. Carter. Nora knows the detective, but she stands by the man who brought me to this place."

The girl did not dream of going to bed.

She went to the window, and found it shuttered like the one in the lower room.

The old house was a prison, which seemed as solid as the Bastille, and at last Margie came away from the window.

An hour passed.

She heard footsteps come up the stairs and stop at the door.

It was Nora coming back to see if she was asleep, and in a few seconds the steps receded.

At last she threw herself upon the bed, and, wearied out, fell into a dreamless slumber.

Suddenly, however, she opened her eyes, and then bounded from the couch.

Smoke which seemed to pour into the room over the door almost suffocated her.

She shrieked for help, she beat the door with her hands, she was here, there, everywhere.

But no help came, and as the walls of the little room grew hot Margie Marne fell senseless and hopeless to the floor.

CHAPTER XXIII.
CARTER AND HIS QUARRY.

It looked like a diabolical plot to make way with the girl who had interested herself in the death of Mother Flintstone.

Margie cried again for help, but none seemed to come.

She heard the roar of flames just beyond the door, and knew that it was locked.

Seconds seemed hours to the doomed maiden, and she felt her strength leave her.

Suddenly there was a crash, and some one broke into the room.

Margie tried to rise, but her powers could not stand the strain, and she fell back once more.

She felt some one lift her from the bed and carry her from the room. She heard voices as in a dream, she felt smoke and flame in her face, and then a rush of cold air.

Was she saved?

Had she been carried from the jaws of death and would she be able to tell the story of her escape?

She did not know.

When she came to again she saw a woman standing over her, and a gentle hand was laid upon her brow.

"It was a narrow escape, child," said the nurse, and Margie looked up with a query in her eyes.

"Tell me," said the girl.

"All I know is that a fireman saved you in the nick of time. He carried you from the house, which was entirely consumed. It was a brave act, and will get him a medal."

"But the woman?"

"They saw no one but you in the house. Was there another?"

"Yes; Nora."

The nurse shook her head.

"The other one may have left the house in time," she remarked.

"She was my jaileress."

"You don't mean to tell me that you were in that house against your will?"

"That's it exactly."

"And you don't know who Nora is?"

"I do not."

Later in the day Margie, now fully recovered from the shock, was able to sit up, and an officer came to see her.

"The man I want to see is Mr. Carter, the detective. I will talk to him," said the girl, and they telephoned for the detective.

In a short time the answer came back that the detective could not be found, and Margie adhered to her declaration that she would talk to no one but him.

Meantime Carter, whom we left in the corridor of the tall building with a revolver at his head, had had an adventure of his own.

Eager to discover something about the man who had lost a card in Mother Flintstone's den, he had made his way to the building, only to reach the third floor, where he was met by a man who covered him and told him that another step would seal his doom.

The detective had not bargained for an adventure of this kind, and the threat took him unawares. He could see the well-built figure of the speaker, though it was not too well revealed, but the man's face seemed to be half concealed by a mask.

He stood but a few feet from the detective, and Nick noticed that the hand which held the weapon did not quiver.

There was a desperate man behind the six-shooter.

"What do you want?" suddenly demanded the stranger.

"I want to see you."

"Well, I'm here."

"George Richmond, we have not met for some time."

The stranger laughed.

"George Richmond, eh? You don't take me for that worthy, do you?"

"You are that man and no one else," was the reply. "I am here to tell you this in spite of the menace of the revolver."

"Well, what do you want with George Richmond?"

Nicholas Carter waved his hand toward a door near the man, and continued:

"You live in this building. We cannot talk in this hall."

"That's right. Come this way, sir."

For the first time the weapon was lowered, and the man called George Richmond by the detective opened the door.

His action revealed a room scantily furnished, but Carter stepped forward.

The moment he crossed the threshold the door was shut, and the other turned a key in the lock.

"Now, sir, what is it?" he demanded.

The detective turned and looked him in the face.

"You have been to Hell's Kitchen," said the detective, as coolly as if he addressed a man in the chief's private room, instead of where he was.

"That's news to me," laughed the listener, as his face seemed to lose color. "What business would I have in that delectable locality?"

"Never mind that. You went there."

"Who says so?"

"The person who saw you."

"You?"

"The person who saw you," repeated the detective, with emphasis, as he watched the man like a hawk.

"Well, what of it?"

"You sounded the walls."

"In Hell's Kitchen?"

"Yes, in Mother Flintstone's den."

"Why, she's dead."

"That's true. You went to her house and sounded the walls. You examined the floor and looked closely at the ceiling."

The fellow seemed to grow desperate.

"What if I did?" he growled.

"You lost something there."

The man started.

"Don't you know that a man bent on evil always leaves a clew behind?"

"That's an old story, but they don't always do that. In the first place, you have nothing to prove that I went to Mother Flintstone's den. I defy you."

One of Carter's hands vanished into a pocket, and came out with a small card between thumb and finger.

"You left this there," said he, coolly, displaying the bit of pasteboard.

The other fastened his eyes upon the card for a moment, and then glared at Carter.

"Supposing all this is true," he said; "what are you going to make out of it?"

"You went there after something the old woman is supposed to have concealed in the den. That is why you searched the walls, George Richmond. Did you do it for your friend, or was it all done on your own hook?"

"For my friend?"

"Yes, for the friend you serve—the money king's heir."

At this there was a sudden start, and Richmond looked toward the door.

"You are taking desperate chances in order to keep up your reputation as a detective," he said at last. "I never thought you would resort to this. I know you. I know that you are Nick Carter, the detective, but with all your shrewdness you can't hoodwink me."

With this the speaker moved toward the door and laid his hand upon the knob.

Before Carter could cross the room he saw the door flung open, and the man sprang out into the hall.

The portal was slammed in Carter's face, and a key turned in the lock.

All this was the work of a second, and he heard the feet of the other on the stairs without.

As for himself, he was a prisoner in the room.

The gas burning overhead revealed the place to him, and he went back and stood for a little while at the table.

He felt that Richmond was already on the street below and out of sight.

"I must follow that villain," said Nick, and again he was at the door.

All his strength could not move the portal, and then he threw himself against it, but still it would not yield.

Other doors had fallen before his assaults, but this one seemed built of adamant, and he drew back out of breath, but by no means discouraged.

He knew he was in the third story of a building, and that the room looked out upon a narrow alleyway between two houses. This he could see from the window, and he saw, too, that he could not reach the fire escape from where he was without great risk.

But it was not his intention to remain in the room any longer than he could help it.

He raised the sash and measured the distance to the fire escape, upon which he would be safe.

The detective studied the situation for a short time, and then dexterously leaped for the escape.

His hands caught the irons, and he drew himself upon the platform.

There he stopped a little while for breath and looked around.

No one seemed to have witnessed his feat, and he congratulated himself in silence that so far he had succeeded almost beyond his expectations.

In another minute he was going down the iron rungs of the ladder with the escaping villain in his mind.

By that time George Richmond was far away, but the detective hoped still to overhaul him.

He gained the street, none the worse for his startling adventure, but, of course, the quarry was gone.

A few yards distant on a corner with the lamplight falling upon his figure stood a policeman, and Carter went toward him.

The copper had seen a man pass a short time before, and told Nick so.

"He went that way a little fast," said the policeman, pointing down the street, and as Carter started off a carriage came around the corner.

The light for a moment fell upon it, and the detective caught sight of a man's face at the window.

He knew it at once—the face of Claude Lamont!

CHAPTER XXIV.
STARTLING DEVELOPMENTS.

Just what the millionaire's son was doing in that part of the city at that hour Carter could not conceive, but that his mission was not of the most honest kind he did not doubt.

The carriage was out of sight in a few moments, and the detective was alone with the patrolman.

Seeing that it was not worth while trying to find Richmond in that locality, the detective made his way to his own quarters near Broadway.

The moment he opened the door he was surprised to see Billy, the street waif, spring from a couch in one corner of the room and bound toward him.

"I've got him located now!" cried the boy.

"You've got who located, Billy?"

"The man who gave me the slip the other night on the street."

"Where is he?"

Billy told the detective that if he would follow him he would show him the man in question, and Nick obeyed.

"Look at the gentleman over there at the table in the corner," said the boy, when he had taken Carter to a little theater and from a secluded spot in the gallery pointed to a man at a table on the ground floor.

"That's Claude Lamont. This is luck, Billy! When did you see him come here?"

"Half an hour ago."

"Well, I'll take care of him now."

The detective sat down and watched the man below.

The place was a free-and-easy, and the resort of a good many shady people, but on that particular night it did not seem to enjoy its usual custom.

The detective could easily believe that Claude Lamont could have been driven to the free-and-easy after he saw his face in the cab, and now he intended to keep the young fellow in sight.

For an hour Carter kept his post, when Claude suddenly arose and looked at his watch.

In another moment he spoke to a man near the table and that person nodded.

Nick left his seat and kept an eye on the nabob's son.

Claude coolly lit a cigar at the counter and moved toward the street.

On the sidewalk he looked both ways and then started off.

Carter was at his heels.

Lamont walked several squares and then turned up the steps of a well-to-do house.

The detective drew back.

Soon after the door had been shut a light appeared in the front window.

Almost at the same time the door of the adjoining house opened slightly and a face peeped out.

"Heavens! Bristol Clara!" cried the detective the moment he spied this face. "Things are playing into my hands better than I deserve. I wonder if she will serve me now."

The door had barely shut ere Carter was there and his ring caused it to open again.

There was a slight cry from the woman in the hall, and the detective pushed in and faced her.

"You?" cried the woman, falling back. "You said you would never bother me again."

"That's true, Clara, but this is for the last time. Who is your neighbor?"

"Ha! don't you know?"

"If I did I wouldn't ask you, would I?"

"Perhaps not. You want to find out something about them?"

"There are two, eh?"

"Yes; one just came home."

"Which one, woman?"

"The one with the dust."

"The other is the featherless bird, is he?"

"Yes, but he's the coolest one, I'm thinking."

"You don't live here for nothing, Clara. This is a sort of double house."

"That's just what it is."

"Then, you know how to see what is going on in the side over there. I want to see, too."

The woman moved across the room and was followed by the detective.

"What's the case now? Tell me that first," said Bristol Clara, stopping suddenly and turning upon the detective.

"Murder."

The woman started.

"Is it that bad?" she exclaimed. "Who was the victim—man or woman?"

"One of your sex."

"Old or young?"

"An old woman—a 'fence,' Clara."

"Not——"

Bristol Clara stopped and looked away.

"I guess you've heard about the crime," said the detective. "I am on the trail of the murderer of Mother Flintstone."

"I thought so. Well, the secret may be in that house beyond this partition. Those men have talked about that very crime. I've heard them."

The woman led the detective upstairs and opened a small door in one of the walls.

A dark apartment was disclosed, and she entered, followed by the man at her heels.

"We are now in the other house," said Clara, laying her hand on the detective's arm, which she found in the dark. "Here is a stairway which I accidentally discovered last summer, and which I have used on several occasions."

"It leads down to the room where I saw the light, doesn't it?"

"Not exactly. There is a hole in the ceiling. I made it with a knife. You see, I didn't know how soon I would be wanting to find out something about my neighbors, so I haven't been idle."

"You're worth your weight in gold, Clara."

In a little while Carter found himself in another dark place, and Clara pointed to a ray of light that seemed to come up from some place under their feet, and the detective drew closer.

"Put your eye down to it," said the woman.

This Nick did, and soon became accustomed to the scene beneath him.

He was looking into a large and expensively furnished room.

Pictures in large gilt frames were arranged on the walls, and thick Brussels carpet covered the floor.

The chandeliers were of expensive make, and everything betokened great wealth.

The room was inhabited at the time by a man who reclined in an armchair under the main light.

Carter knew him at once.

It was Claude Lamont.

The detective had a good chance to study the young man's features, and he could note how eager he seemed to greet some one. He was not kept long in suspense when the door leading to the main hall opened and some one entered.

"George Richmond—my old friend," smiled Nick, as he watched the other one. "He gave me the slip in the tall building, and now greets his old chum, Claude."

"You're a little behind," said Claude, looking at his friend. "You must have had an adventure."

"That's just what I've had," laughed the other, taking a cigar from the open box on the table at Lamont's elbow. "Say I didn't play it on the shrewdest old ferret in the city, will you?"

"On a detective? What, have you had a bout with one of those people?"

"Haven't I? I left him in durance, and it will be some time before he gets out, I'm thinking."

"Come, tell the whole story. I've had a little adventure myself," exclaimed Lamont. "You don't mean to say that you've had a little episode with our friend Carter?"

"With no one else."

"Why didn't you silence him?"

"I hardly know. But we'll fix him later on."

"Did he know you?"

"Yes."

"What gave you away?"

"One of my old cards. I lost it in the den."

"Oh, you've been back there, eh?"

"Yes. I went back to give the old place another inspection. I sounded the walls and inspected the floor, but I couldn't find the papers."

"Then they don't exist."

"I'm beginning to think that way myself. But the old hag certainly knew the truth, and don't you think she made out just such papers intending to leave them some day to the girl or to the street rat?"

"To the girl perhaps, but never to the rat," said Lamont. "Margie knows a good deal, and would be a dangerous person for us to fight if she had the cleverness of some women. But she's caged for some time, and Nora will see that she remains silent. But the papers? We must have something of the kind. If Mother Flintstone did not leave such, we must make them."

"Now, that's it."

"The governor won't knuckle down till he sees them, and then we'll get all we want."

For half a second Richmond smoked in silence, and then he threw away his cigar.

"We must make the papers!" he cried. "Your father, Perry Lamont, must give you free use of his purse strings. When I called on him and threatened to send you to the gallows unless he handed over ten thousand dollars he laughed in my face, and I came away with no cash at all. But I picked a check book from the desk, as you know, with one good check filled out. That's helped us some."

"Yes; but it's a mere drop in the bucket. The governor must be confronted with certain papers proving that Mother Flintstone was his sister and my aunt. That will open the cash box, I guess!"

And young Lamont laughed.

"The infernal villains!" ejaculated Carter, as these details of infamy fell upon his ears; "if that isn't a gallows pair then I never saw one in all my life. Claude Lamont can't get his hands on the Lamont cash box, and that's what worries him. One of those men killed Mother Flintstone; but which one?"

In another moment Claude and Richmond arose and left the room, and Bristol Clara said:

"That ends the exhibition for the present," and the detective answered that he was satisfied.

CHAPTER XXV.
A TERRIBLE COMPACT.

Perry Lamont, the millionaire, stood underneath the brilliant chandelier in his luxurious library, apparently waiting for some one. He looked anxiously toward the door, and when it opened his eyes glittered.

The person who entered the room was his son.

For half a second father and son stood face to face, and then the former waved the other to a chair.

Claude, looking a little worse for the night out, complied, and waited for his father to speak.

"Who is this man Richmond?" asked Lamont, senior.

The young man started.

"He is your friend, I believe?"

"He is, and he is a nice gentleman," said Claude.

"I judge so," and a smile came to the father's lips.

"What has happened? You speak sarcastically this morning."

"Do I? Well, I want you to give up this 'nice gentleman.'"

Claude looked away, but in a moment his gaze came back to his father's face.

"This man is a rascal," spoke up the millionaire.

"That's a pretty bold charge against a friend of mine."

"Bold or not, it's true."

"Who is the accuser?"

"Never mind that."

"I demand to know. Mr. Richmond has a right to face his accuser, and he will do so."

"But you haven't denied the charge of your friend."

"I do it now."

"Then he is a nice gentleman still, is he?"

"He is, sir."

Claude flushed.

"I am the accuser," and the face of the millionaire grew white. "I call him a rascal."

"Upon what grounds?"

"He tried to blackmail me."

"Mr. Richmond?"

"Yes, sir. That man came here but a few days ago and wanted to rob me of ten thousand dollars."

"Impossible!" cried Claude, feigning astonishment.

"It is true, and what is more, he hinted that you had committed a great crime."

"Come, come; you must have been dreaming."

"I was as wide awake then as I am now."

Lamont, senior, smiled knowingly.

"You must drop this black bird."

"I am of age and have the right to choose my friends," was his son's answer.

"Then keep him and yourself in the future."

The young man gazed at his father in wide-open astonishment.

"You certainly don't mean that," he said.

"I do. He is your friend, you say. Keep him and yourself. I guess that's plain."

Claude Lamont arose and crossed the room.

"You don't know what you do," he cried.

"I know what I do. It is either lose this friend, as you call him, or lose your fortune."

"He never tried to blackmail you."

"He did!" thundered the nabob. "In this very room he wanted to sell the so-called secret for ten thousand dollars. I drove him away. I wouldn't have anything to do with the scoundrel. But it seems you do. You are with him night and day, and you are old enough to know that you can't play with pitch and not become defiled."

Claude smiled derisively at this, and for a moment was silent.

"Look here," he suddenly said, "I can't give this man up. He knows too much."

"What's that?" cried Lamont, senior. "Do you admit that you are in his power?"

"I didn't say so. I only remarked that I can't throw him to one side. He knows too much."

"Against whom?"

"Against the house."

"It cannot be."

"I'm afraid it's true. This man is my friend, and I have been keeping near him for a purpose, and that purpose the salvation of the good name of Lamont."

A strange and eager light seemed to come into the millionaire's eyes, and for half a second he did not continue.

"Sit down," he said. "Tell me what this man knows."

Claude went back to the chair.

"He knows a good deal more than we can afford to let him tell," he said. "I don't say that Richmond will tell the secret on the street or anything of that kind, but we can't afford to let him have the opportunity."

"In God's name, what is the secret?"

"Of course he never told me, but I only guess at it from hints he has dropped while in his cups. It's a terrible thing, if it's true—a fearful secret, father."

"Out with it. I am strong, you see, and can listen to any recital you make."

Claude crossed the room, and looked cautiously into the hall.

No one was there.

Coming back, he resumed his seat in the chair and looked at the white-faced man opposite.

"Whatever became of Aunt Hester?" he asked.

The expression that came into Perry Lamont's face was most startling.

Every vestige of color left it, and it became as white as a marble statue.

"Who ever told you that I had a sister named Hester?" he asked.

"Never mind that. I only asked the question."

"Is this some of your friend's work?"

"That is a part of his secret. He says he has certain papers that will startle the world, that he has in his possession a certain confession or a family history written out by an old woman who called herself——"

Young Lamont paused, for his father was gasping like a man fighting for his breath.

"Go on. Tell me all. What did this woman call herself?" he cried.

"Mother Flintstone," coolly said the son. "She lived in Hell's Kitchen, and after being threatened a number of times—in spite of the protection of Carter's assistants—she was murdered a few nights ago."

"Yes, yes. I saw something of that in the newspapers."

"Well, from what I have heard Richmond say in a dark way when in his cups he can prove that Mother Flintstone, the old fence, was your sister."

"Great heavens!" cried Perry Lamont. "Has he got the documents left by this woman?"

"I fear he has."

"But he didn't offer them to me."

"I can't say as to that."

"He only offered to keep the knowledge of your doings from the world for ten thousand dollars."

"But he has the papers now. I am confident of that."

"Will he sell them?" eagerly asked the millionaire.

"He might."

"For how much?"

"You must negotiate with him."

"Look here, Claude, my boy. Can't you get possession of those papers?"

"How?"

"Any way, I don't care how you get them."

"You wouldn't want me to rob my friend?"

"I say I don't care how you get them."

"But he would still possess the secret."

"We'll take care of him after the documents have been found. How did he get them? Was he familiar with Mother Flintstone?"

- 178 -

"I don't know."

"Merciless villain! He holds the peace of our house in his hands. The man is the quintessence of rascality. Talk about your polished blackmailers. He stands at the head of the procession. I'll hand him over to the police at once."

"Try it, and the whole thing will come out."

Lamont, senior, gasped again.

"Where does Richmond board?"

"He changes his place often. I don't believe he sleeps two nights in the same place."

"Like the sultan. But, look here, my boy. You don't want the good name of our house destroyed?"

"One of the last things I want to see," said the young rake.

"Then help me destroy this man. Help me to get those papers and silence him."

"It is true, then?"

"It is true."

"Mother Flintstone was your sister?"

"Yes, yes. She was Hester, the sister who contracted a poor marriage years ago and finally drifted into crime."

Claude Lamont seemed struck with a thunderbolt, and for some time he sat in the presence of his father, dazed and speechless.

"I had hoped the truth would never come out," continued the millionaire. "I accidentally discovered a year ago who Mother Flintstone was, but I said nothing. I would have given her thousands to have thrown herself from the bridge or to have left the city, but I dared not approach her. And so she left a confession behind; she has left the secret to a scoundrel like this George Richmond. Why, this man has more names than one."

"A good many people have nowadays," answered Claude.

"Well, he must be silenced somehow."

"With money?"

"Not if I can help it. I would like to know what sort of communication Mother Flintstone left."

"It seems to me the best way to deal with the secret holder is to come to his terms," suggested Claude.

"And be bled every now and then? I'll defy him first!"

"Come, come. You can't afford to do that. Think of our station in society. Sister is on the eve of marriage, and mother's health is not what it used to be. We must come to his terms to save the house of Lamont."

The millionaire began to pace the floor like a wild beast.

"What will you take to strangle the scoundrel, Claude?" he suddenly exclaimed, halting before his son. "You have every opportunity. Name your price."

"You don't really mean that?" cried the young man.

"I do, every word of it. What will you take to silence this man forever?"

"Two hundred thousand cash in hand."

"Done!" exclaimed the millionaire. "That's a bargain!"

CHAPTER XXVI.
THE DARK JAILERESS AGAIN.

It was a cool compact.

Perry Lamont made answer to his son with all the cleverness of a practiced villain, and Claude accepted it in the same manner.

"I want this man silenced," continued the millionaire. "He must not possess this secret."

"Just as you say," said Claude, picking up a cigar and coolly lighting it.

"He must not, I say. You've agreed to finish him, and when you've done so the money is yours."

"Couldn't you give me a little check now?" asked the son.

Perry Lamont took a check book from the desk and opened it as he looked at his son.

"How much?"

"Say five thousand. I may need the money in the venture, you know."

Without more ado the nabob drew up a check for five thousand dollars, and passed it across the table.

"This business must not lag," said he. "While that man lives he is dangerous."

Five minutes later the young man stood on a corner in another part of the city. He was smoking complacently and apparently waiting for some one, for he watched the door of a well-known resort.

Presently the door opened and George Richmond came out.

Claude joined him at once, and the pair walked away together.

In a little while they seated themselves at a table in a room not far from the corner, and Claude threw the check upon the table.

"Jehu! did you make it?" cried Richmond.

"I did."

"How?"

The young scamp smiled.

"It's blood money," he said.

"Blood money?" exclaimed Richmond. "In Heaven's name, whose blood does it mean?"

"Yours!"

"Come, what joke is this?"

"It is no joke. I never joke on serious matters like this."

The eyes of the two men met.

"This check is signed by your father, and yet you tell me that it is blood money."

"That's precisely what it is. He's hired me to kill you."

George Richmond broke into a laugh and leaned back in his chair.

"You don't look like it, boy," he cried. "Well, if I'm to be killed, why don't you do it now?"

Claude reached forward and picked up the check.

"I'm to have a cool two hundred thousand for the job," said he. "Just think of it! You're an important person."

"Hang me if I ain't. Why does the old man want me out of the way?"

"You hold the secret, and he believes you have the papers left by Mother Flintstone."

"You gave him that gaff, did you?"

"Yes, in great shape."

"I hardly thought you'd do it. But since you have I suppose you're to furnish proofs that I've been killed."

"Of course."

"You are not expected to furnish the corpse, I hope?"

"No; not quite that. But he's to have some sort of proofs, and then we'll get the two hundred thousand."

For an hour these men kept their heads together and talked in low tones.

They discussed first one plan and then another, and when they at last adjourned and stepped out upon the street they seemed satisfied about something.

Not far from the place of meeting a hand was laid upon Claude Lamont's arm, and he looked into the face of a tall woman.

"You?" he cried, for he was alone, having separated from Richmond a few moments previous.

"Yes? Why not?"

"I thought I left you in the nest with Margie."

"So you did, but there isn't any nest now."

"No nest? What's happened?"

"The old place is in ashes."

Lamont uttered a startled cry, and looked at the woman, who did not speak.

"You weren't to hurt the girl, you know?" said he.

"That's true, but I couldn't help it."

"But tell me. Come in here. No one will listen to us. Now, what has taken place?"

Nora took a long breath and began.

"The girl got almost unruly. I got her up to bed, but she faced me and threatened."

"Well, you shouldn't have paid any attention to her words."

"I couldn't help it. She mentioned a name that drove every vestige of color from my face."

"An old enemy's name, eh?"

"Yes; she spoke of a detective whom I fear with all my soul. She spoke of Carter."

"And made you chicken-hearted, eh? Pshaw, woman!"

"I couldn't help it, I say. It filled me with fear, and I broke away."

"Well?"

"By and by the room became still, and I found that she was asleep at last."

"That's good."

"In the room below I upset the lamp."

"The devil you did, woman! You must have been badly frightened."

"I was. In an instant it seemed the fire was everywhere. I saw it mount the stairs and dart toward the girl's room. Fear almost paralyzed me. I tried to get upstairs, but failed. The fire was everywhere. It filled the whole house, it seemed. I could no more stop its progress than I could stop the river yonder. I fled for my life."

"And left Margie to perish in the flames?"

"Got help me, I did."

Lamont leaned back and looked at the woman, whose face was deathly white.

"Did she perish?" he asked at last.

"She must have died in the old house. I did not stay to look after her. Fear lent speed to my limbs, and I ran like a deer. Not for the world would I have gone back."

"You've killed the girl!" hissed Claude Lamont. "You've made a murderess out of yourself."

Nora did not speak, but looked into the young man's face and exposed anew the whiteness of her own.

"I suppose you haven't been there since?" he said.

"What, go back to that spot? Never!"

Claude Lamont drained the glass at his elbow and seemed to take a long breath.

"What makes you fear this man, Carter? What did he ever do that gives you the chills?"

"That's my secret," cried the woman, half defiantly.

"What makes him your enemy, and, pray, what did you do that his name terrifies you?"

She did not answer him.

"Look here!" suddenly said Claude. "If you've killed the girl by your faint heart I'll hold you responsible."

"Just as you please," was the reply.

Nora seemed to be getting her old nerve back, for she spoke with spirit, and her cheeks flushed for the first time.

"You never got such orders from me," he went on.

"I know it. I dropped the lamp——"

"Come, no excuses," interrupted the young man. "I shall hold you responsible—guilty of murder."

"Just as if you never did anything that has a shady side," hissed the woman. "You're a nice man to talk thus. What have you done that makes an angel out of you, I should like to know?"

"No accusations, woman."

"Very well. Will you hand me over to the police? Will you tell the inspector that I am the last person who saw the girl alive? I guess not!"

"Don't dare me."

"What if I tell them that Margie was Mother Flintstone's granddaughter——"

"She wasn't!" flashed Claude Lamont.

"You take it up in a jiffy," grinned Nora. "If she wasn't why did you resent my words so soon?"

For half a second Lamont watched the dark face before him, and then he said:

"We'll call it quits. After all, perhaps you couldn't have helped it. The lamp fell from your hand, did it?"

"I told you once."

"And you couldn't stop the flames?"

"I couldn't. I'd give my eyes if that girl was alive to-day. I did not do it intentionally. My evil genius must have been on the watch."

"We'll say so, at any rate, Nora."

It was the first time he had spoken her name during the interview, and his voice was considerably softened.

"The department may have reached the fire in time to save the girl," he went on.

"No, no! she perished. The whole house was in flames by the time I got away. I'm going now."

"Still afraid of the detective's shadow?"

"Never mind the detective. I'm going, I say."

"Do you mean that you're going away?"

"Yes—to put ten thousand miles between me and that infernal crime of mine."

Lamont drew forth his pocketbook and began to count out some bills.

"Put up your money. It's blood money!" cried Nora. "I wouldn't touch a penny of your father's wealth. I don't want money. I've got all I shall need."

"Then you're going but a short distance?"

"Yes; not far."

The last word seemed to come from between clenched teeth, and a desperate look settled on the woman's face.

"Then here's to you, Nora, and good luck go with you," and Lamont held out his hand.

She pushed it away, with a look of disdain.

"It's like your money. There's blood on it, too!" she exclaimed. "Some day you'll wish you had never had anything to do with this game of crime. Good-by."

She sprang up, gave him another look and vanished.

"She's mad, but it's all right. She will try the river," he laughed.

CHAPTER XXVII.
FOUND IN THE TIDE.

After the scene the detective had witnessed through Bristol Clara's assistance he made his way to another part of the city and entered a little house, where he was confronted by Billy, the street rat.

The detective wanted to ascertain if the boy had picked up anything new, and his first words startled him.

"They didn't burn her up, Mr. Carter."

"Didn't burn who up, Billy?"

"Margie, you know."

The detective as yet had heard nothing of the fire at which Margie Marne nearly lost her life, and he lost no time questioning Billy.

The boy had heard of the fire through a fireman, and had gone direct to the hospital, where he had held an interview with the girl herself.

"I'll see her, too," said Nick. "This is important, Billy, and Margie must be seen."

Imagine the astonishment of the girl when she saw Carter walking up the aisle toward her.

A smile of pleasure overspread her face, and she held out her hand.

"This is indeed a great pleasure," cried Margie. "We've been sending after you, and just when we give you up here you come. I've been within the shadow of death."

"So Billy told me."

"I wonder if Nora, my jaileress, escaped?"

"We will find that out by and by. Tell me the whole story, Margie, and then we will see what can be done."

The girl proceeded, and gave the detective the entire story of her adventures while in the hands of Claude Lamont and under Nora's care, and Nick listened attentively.

"I think I can locate your jaileress," said he, at the end of Margie's narrative.

"Do so. She didn't treat me badly, only she was true to her master. She started at the mention of your name, though."

"Did she?" smiled Carter.

"It drove every vestige of color from her face."

"She's met me somewhere, then," said the detective. "I want to see Nora."

Half an hour later the detective reached the scene of the fire, and looked upon the ruins of Margie's prison.

The house had been entirely destroyed, and some of the neighbors seemed glad that it was so.

"None of us liked the tall, dark-faced woman, with the little, red scar over her left eye," said a woman who lived near the place, and whom the detective addressed.

"What did you call her?"

"Oh, we never called on her at all. She was very exclusive."

"Had no visitors, eh?"

"Yes, sometimes. A man would drop in, generally after dark, and stay about half an hour."

"You saw him, did you?"

"I couldn't help it, you see, from where I live."

"What was he like?"

"He was younger than the woman. He was always well dressed, like a swell nabob, and carried himself like a sport."

"Claude again," thought Carter. "You never saw the woman go out?"

His last question was addressed to the neighbor.

"Not often. She remained at home, and seemed to attend to her own business."

"You're sure about that scar, are you?"

"Bless you, yes. I saw it more than once, when we happened to meet in the little grocery on the corner yonder. It was a real, red scar."

Carter handed the woman a piece of money, which she did not refuse, and went away. He went direct to police headquarters and to the famous rogues' gallery.

There he began to look through the large albums containing the faces of criminals and suspects, and for nearly an hour he turned the thick leaves industriously.

At last he stopped and leaned over the page.

His eyes seemed to become fastened upon a certain face, that of a woman, angular and dark.

Turning to the proper entry he read a description of the woman whose photographed face was before him, and he seemed to smile when he noted that she had a brilliant red scar over the left eye.

"This must be our old friend," said the detective. "This is Mag Maginnis, the shoplifter, whom I sent up the river five years ago. I didn't see the scar then. She got it since, and the photograph is the second one she's had the honor of having in this collection. So Mag started at mention of my name by Margie. No wonder. I filled her with terror when I caught her in the dry-goods district in the very act of plundering a counter. We'll see."

He shut the album and walked away.

The detective never let a trail get cold, and therefore he proceeded to a part of the city where he hoped to strike Mag's trail.

"The Lord deliver us! Here's Mr. Carter!" cried a woman's shrill voice, as the detective opened a door and confronted a female at a table.

The woman had seen better days, for an air of refinement still lingered about the place, the appointments of which were poor.

She sat bolt upright, looking into the face she had instantly recognized, and the detective stood for a moment at the door.

"You don't want me, I hope?" asked the woman.

"Not at all, Sybil."

"That's good, but I couldn't see how you would, seeing that I've been good for three years."

"I know that, and you're to have all the credit, too."

"Thank you, Mr. Carter. But if you had come a little sooner you might have seen an old friend," and the woman laughed.

"What old friend was here, Sybil?"

"It was Mag. You remember her?"

In spite of his coolness the detective started.

"Yes," continued the woman called Sybil, "Mag was here, and bade me good-by. She's going off. What's happened, Mr. Carter? Mag wouldn't explain."

"Where did she go, Sybil?" asked the detective, paying no attention to the woman's query.

"She did not tell me. But I never saw Mag in just the way she was. She said she was tired of life, tired of pulling other people's chestnuts out of the fire, and now and then she acted like a person on the verge of insanity. She may have gone to the river, for once or twice she mentioned it in despairing tones."

"How long has she been gone?" eagerly questioned the detective.

"Barely twenty minutes."

"I'll see you later, Sybil," cried the detective, turning to the door. "I must find Mag, if possible."

"She's Nora now, you know."

"Yes, yes."

"She dropped 'Mag' months ago, or soon after she came down the river."

"But she's Mag yet," smiled Carter, and in another second the woman was left alone wondering why he wanted to see Nora so badly.

There were many chances against Nick finding the woman he sought, but he did not despair.

The piers of New York are many and long.

From them thousands have leaped to their death, or been thrown into the waters after dark by those whose hands are red with crime.

More than once the detective's trail had taken him to the docks, and there he had picked up more than one clew.

Every dock in the city was known to Carter.

While among them he was at home, and knew where they began and ended.

The bare thought that this old criminal had gone to the river in a fit of remorse, for he doubted not that she thought Margie had perished in the fire, urged him on.

Of course, if Nora intended to commit suicide she had had ample time to carry out her plans, but still there was a chance that she had changed her mind.

The detective reached the river at a spot nearest the house he had just left.

He could see nothing of the hunted woman, and no crowd such as gathers on the piers when the body of a suicide has been discovered greeted him.

The detective walked along the river front for some distance with his senses on the alert.

All at once he caught sight of something floating in the water, and he stopped suddenly and leaned forward.

It did not take him long to see that the object was the body of a woman, and Carter called a policeman who stood a short distance away.

"That's the same woman!" cried the patrolman the moment he caught sight of the body.

"What woman?" asked Carter.

"Why, sir, the woman who came down here three hours ago and asked me some fool questions about the river."

"Well?"

"I didn't notice which way she went. But that's her."

Nick and the policeman managed to bring the body against the logs of the pier, and the detective clambered down and hauled it up.

The burden was a heavy one, but the detective's hand did not lose its grip, and in time the body lay on the wharf, which it drenched.

The detective looked into the long face, and his gaze alighted upon a little scar over the left eye.

"This is Nora—Margie's jaileress, but she's Mag Maginnis, the old offender. She's not to blame entirely for this. The hand of her master drove her to suicide, and he shall pay for it!"

Carter seemed to speak the last words through clenched teeth, and his voice told that he meant every word he said.

The policeman in the meantime called the patrol, and Nick had extracted from the woman's bosom a little flat package like a memorandum, which he hastily transferred to his own pocket.

"That's the end of one poor, storm-tossed soul," muttered the detective as he walked away. "I found Mag sooner than I expected, but we've not heard the last of her."

Half a block from the river front the detective nearly ran against a man who came out of a house with a reputation none of the best and walked off.

The walk and the well-known shoulders as revealed by the man caused a light of recognition to leap up into Carter's eyes, and his gaze followed the fellow some distance.

"What brought you to the scene of Nora's death, Claude Lamont?" mentally queried the man of clews. "Did you have to hound the poor creature to the last terrible act of her life?"

CHAPTER XXVIII.
A FAIR FOE.

The detective followed the young man until he lost him beyond the doors of a well-known café, and then he turned away.

Nora, alias Mag Maginnis, had ended her life in the cold waters of the river, and the detective believed that Claude Lamont was morally responsible.

"Now for another visit to the lion's den," said Carter, as he made his way to another part of the city and rang the bell attached to the millionaire's mansion.

It was not the hour for a social call, but he found the money king at home. He had not forgotten his former visit, when he was faced by the daughter and warned not to carry his hunt too far.

Carter still saw the fine figure of the girl before him and her flashing eyes, but she had not deterred him.

He was shown at once to the library, and Perry Lamont turned his chair so as to face the detective.

"What is it, sir?" he asked.

Before Carter could reply the door opened and the daughter, Opal, came in.

Opal Lamont was handsome, with a fine figure and a bright face; but her eyes seemed full of fire, and unnatural fire at that.

Spying the detective, she advanced haughtily and faced him.

"Are you going to hold an interview with this man?" she asked her father.

"I presume he is here to see me."

"I'll remain," answered Opal, and the next moment she dropped into a chair and turned her face to the detective.

Her manner was positive, if not insulting, and the detective swallowed it mutely.

Perry Lamont seemed rejoiced to have his daughter beside him.

It made him look triumphantly at Carter, and for a moment a smile of victory appeared at his mouth.

"Now, sir, we'll proceed," he said. "Your mission here you can make known and we will listen."

"You remember that I am on the trail of the person who killed Mother Flintstone?"

"I remember."

"You remember, too, begging the young lady's pardon, that the old lady was your near kin."

These words were like a spark to a magazine, and the next moment Opal broke forth:

"It's the same old blackmailing scheme, father. You shall not listen to it."

"Calm yourself, Miss Lamont——"

"I am calm enough now. You shall not introduce such subjects in this house. We do not recognize the old hag who was killed, perhaps righteously, in the place called Hell's Kitchen. You must talk about another matter if you want to remain here."

Perry Lamont looked crushed and almost helpless in his chair.

He glanced at his daughter, and then toward the door leading into the hall.

"Where's Claude?" he asked.

"He is not in just now," answered Opal.

"No, sir," put in the detective. "Your son just now is not in; but I could enlighten you as to his whereabouts."

"You've been playing spy, have you?"

"I've been following the trail of one who has been your brother's friend, miss."

Opal Lamont colored and for half a second remained silent.

"It is blackmail all the same," she resumed at last. "In the first place, whatever that old woman was to us we don't intend to be bled."

"I believe you once offered me ten thousand dollars not to pursue this trail, miss."

"I did it for his sake," and she nodded toward her father. "I don't want his nerves shattered."

The detective glanced at Perry Lamont and pitied the abject old figure in the chair.

"They looked alike," was all he said, with a glance at Miss Opal.

The daughter curled her lip and looked away.

"Never mind," she said. "My day will come, Mr. Detective."

Carter turned once more to the millionaire and said:

"I'll state my business. I am here to ask you about that contract."

Lamont started.

"What contract?" he asked.

"The one you made with your son."

There was a cry and a sudden start, and the millionaire nearly fell from his chair.

"I made no contract!" he cried.

"None whatever?"

"None!"

"You did not promise him a large sum if he would put a certain person out of the way?"

"I did not."

"That's blackmail, pure and simple," flashed Opal Lamont. "You cannot succeed."

She arose and crossed the room.

Perry Lamont seemed to grovel in his chair.

"You deny the contract, do you?" queried the detective.

"I do."

"He never lies!" exclaimed the girl.

"And never forgets, eh?"

"Never!"

"Then his mind is greatly at fault this minute. Let me ask another question."

"Not another one! He has been questioned enough. Don't you see you have excited him?"

"Not so much but that he can answer intelligently. Perry Lamont, your sister did not die heirless."

"My God!"

"She left some of her blood behind. She did not pass out of the world at the hand of the assassin without leaving behind some one who has a right to her name!"

The look of the millionaire became a stare, and his hand shook as he laid it upon the desk before him.

"Come!" cried Opal. "Must we really buy your silence?"

"It is not in the market, miss, as I have once told you. I want to reach the solution of this terrible crime. I shall not turn from the trail till I am at the end of it. Mother Flintstone's blood calls for revenge, and——"

Opal, who stood beside her father, leaned over him and whispered in his ear.

The old man's face brightened.

"Not another word till I come back," continued the girl to her parent, and with this she left the room.

Two minutes later her steps were heard at the door across the room and once more she stood before Nick.

In that short time she had gowned herself for the street, and, stepping to one side, she touched a button.

"We are going out," said she, looking at the detective. "I have just ordered the carriage."

The detective looked amazed.

Going out with that girl?

The turn of affairs actually amused him.

"I want you to accompany me to a certain place," continued Opal Lamont. "We shall not be there long; but you must go with me."

The detective consented, and in a few moments they entered the carriage which had come to the front door.

Opal had drawn a spotted veil over her face and had fallen back into the depths of the vehicle saying nothing, although addressed by the detective.

The coachman seemed to know where to go.

Carter had not heard the girl give him any orders, but he turned corner after corner, as if his destination was plain to him.

For at least ten minutes the vehicle bounced over the stones, and then it halted in front of a two-story brick house in the lower part of Gotham.

The detective looked out, and took in the contour of the house, and Opal opened the door of the cab.

"We're here," she said, speaking for the first time since leaving home, and in a moment she dismounted, to be followed by the nonplused detective.

The millionaire's daughter led the way up the steps, and with a key opened the front door.

As she threw it back she motioned to the detective to enter, and Carter soon stood in a fireless parlor darkened by heavy curtains at the windows.

"I'll see you in a moment," said Opal, rushing toward the door, and the detective heard the sound of leather and silk on the stairs.

"This is a queer adventure," thought Carter. "This must be one of the many houses Perry Lamont owns. The young woman is a cool-headed thing and seems to have the nerves her father has lost. Why has she brought me to this place? What new mystery is this? Ah! here she comes!"

There were footsteps in the hall, and the detective watched the door.

But the sounds did not seem to come all the way down the flight; they appeared to stop midway, and the detective glanced up at the open transom.

The sight he saw there riveted him to the spot.

Leaning over the banisters was Opal Lamont, but how changed.

Her face was as white as a sheet, and her lips were welded like pieces of steel.

The hat had been discarded, and her long hair fell in uncombed masses over her shoulder.

The girl looked like an avenging spirit, and the detective thought he had never seen a face just like hers.

The whole thing appeared more visionary than real; it seemed some hideous dream in which he was to be the victim, but that it was terrible reality the detective soon discovered.

The lips sprang apart suddenly, and Nick heard the voice of the creature on the stairs.

"I hardly expected to trap you so easily," she said, in sharp, triumphant tones. "You fell into the snare like a tenderfoot. Did you think I was about to reveal something to you? Your time has come! I hold death in my hand, and I haven't practiced at the pistol galleries for nothing."

Carter saw the revolver which Opal Lamont thrust forward; he tried to spring to the door, but some unseen agency seemed to root him to the carpet. Then came a flash, leaping tigerlike through the transom, as it seemed—then darkness.

CHAPTER XXIX.
THE BACK TRAIL.

All this time the carriage which had carried Opal and Carter to the house had waited for the girl just around the nearest corner.

When Opal emerged from the place no excitement was noticed about her.

She walked as gayly as if she had not sent a man to his doom, and when she stepped into the carriage there was a smile on her lips.

She knew what she had done, and the secret was hers.

The vehicle went straight to the Lamont mansion, and the girl dismissed it at the door.

She entered the house and passed directly to her room on one of the upper floors, where she changed her gown; then she descended to the library, where she had left her father.

She found him in the same position at the desk as if he had not stirred since her departure.

He met her eye the moment she entered the room, and she came forward, saying nothing.

"I'm glad to see you back, Opal. Did you get rid of that man?"

"Yes."

"You did not let him blackmail you?"

"I did not."

"You did not——"

Perry Lamont stopped as if he was on dangerous ground, but Opal could not avoid his gaze.

Her eyes seemed to betray her.

"You surely did not——" began the millionaire again, but stopped as before.

"Never mind where he is," put in Opal. "I'm quite sure Nick Carter will not give us any more trouble."

"That's good. I'm glad to hear you say that, and your manner convinces me that it is so. I trust he didn't give you any trouble, child?"

"None in the least. There, don't bother about that man. He's out of the way; won't trouble you any more."

Opal arose and swept from the room, the eyes of the nabob following her with mute questioning.

He heard her on the floor above, and closed his eyes as he leaned back in the chair.

Did he suspect the truth?

Did the rich man dream that his child had handled a revolver within the last hour, and that she had aimed at a man's breast?

If he thought of such things he made no sign.

It was some hours after these events that the door of the library was opened and Claude, his son, came in.

Lamont was now fast asleep, and the young sport watched him for ten minutes.

Stealing over to the desk, Claude opened a drawer near his father's hand and extracted a large envelope therefrom.

As he was transferring it to his pocket Opal looked into the room, and then came forward.

"Don't awaken him," she said. "I want to see you, Claude. Come across the hall."

"Mother——"

"Mother won't hear us, for she is lying down overhead. Come with me. I didn't know you were in the house."

"I just came in."

"Good."

The pair left the library and crossed the hall to the darkened parlor, where Opal turned suddenly on her brother.

"Have you done it yet?" she asked.

Claude started in spite of himself.

"Done what?"

"You know. I happened to overhear you and father. Have you finished him?"

"I don't understand you?"

"Oh, yes, you do. You know about the two hundred thousand. You were to get the confession, besides silencing him."

"I've done nothing yet. I understand now," said Claude, with a faint smile.

"When will you?"

"Just as soon as I get a chance."

"Don't you think you're putting it off too long?"

"I don't know. I'm doing my best."

"But while he lives and keeps the confession written in Hell's Kitchen it will be against us."

"Yes."

"You're his chum. You know where he nests, and you are the proper person to silence this man with the terrible secret. You're not afraid of the law, are you?"

Again Claude Lamont started and looked down into the flushed face of his sister.

"No, I'm not afraid of that, but you see I can't strike till I have a fair target."

"I know that."

"There is that bothersome detective," suggested Claude.

"Never mind him," laughed Opal; "he's silenced."

"Since when?"

"Don't ask too many questions. He's silenced, I say."

"I guess not. I've seen him lately."

"When?"

"Yesterday."

"I've got later news than that!" cried the young girl. "I'm right from the seat of war, so to speak."

Claude wanted to ask further questions, but she stopped him by laying her hand on his shoulder.

"That man was an enemy of us all," she said. "He was dangerous, Claude."

"Positively so," was the reply.

"He was a living menace to our future happiness; he was as dangerous as this man Richmond, your friend, and his confession. I shuddered whenever I thought of Nick Carter, who would not let me buy him off."

"He was incorruptible, was he?" laughed Claude.

"Yes, but he's fixed now."

"With whose money, Opal? Father's?"

"With something that silences better than gold," was the startling answer. "I would never face him the second time with a bribe. I know what's what."

"See here. You've got me on nettles. What's become of this man? I demand to know?"

Opal thought a moment, and then turned her head away.

"When have you been to the Cedar Street house?" she asked, without looking at him.

"Not in six months."

"Here's the key. Go and look inside."

"Pshaw! there's nothing there for me."

"You don't know what's there, since you confess that you haven't crossed its threshold in six months."

"If you tell me the secret I won't have to make the trip."

"Go and find it." Opal pushed her brother away. "I want to make sure of a certain thing."

"I see. You've been to the Cedar Street house."

Opal gave him a knowing look, and again pushed him toward the door.

"I'll go, hang me if I don't!" he exclaimed. "I say, sis, if you've intrusted a secret to that house it ought to be safe, for it hasn't been tenanted for half a year. Into which part of it shall I look?"

"In the first room to the right."

"The old-fashioned parlor, eh?"

"Yes, there, there!" cried the millionaire's child. "God forgive me, Claude, I couldn't help it. I had him in the snare."

Five minutes later Claude Lamont stood on the sidewalk in front of his home.

"In creation's name, what does sis mean?" he asked himself. "What has she been doing in that old house? Something desperate, I'll bet my head."

He walked to the first corner, where he took a passing car and rode downtown.

A few minutes later he left it, and proceeded to Cedar Street.

The millionaire owned half a dozen houses there, but the one designated by Opal was the best of all.

With the key supplied by his sister, the city sport let himself into the house and shut the door carefully behind him.

Then he made his way to the first room on the right of the hall and opened its portal.

It was quite dark, all the curtains down—Lamont kept his untenanted houses already furnished—and Claude had to strike a match.

"Jehu! what did sis mean, anyhow?" he exclaimed, as the light flickered up. "No one here."

He held the lucifer above his head and took a survey of the parlor.

Everything seemed in place, and he looked everywhere as he moved about the room.

He noticed that the transom over the hall door was wide open, but he thought nothing of this.

The faintest odor of burned powder assailed his nostrils and he stood in the middle of the room a few seconds and sniffed the air.

"The girl's mad!" he suddenly cried. "What is the fool's errand she wanted me to attend to, I'd like to know? There's nothing in this room, and yet she wanted me to look nowhere else but in this chamber. There's the smell of powder here. What does it mean? She was here, she admitted. She can shoot like a professional. I've seen her at it in the gallery. I'll have to go back and laugh at her foolery."

Claude quitted the room, and, to make sure there was nothing out of the way in the house, went all over it.

"Sis is out of her head," he again exclaimed, when he had inspected the last room. "She may have thought she trapped the detective, but she did nothing of the kind."

When he left the Cedar Street house it was to go straight home.

He peeped into the library, but his father was no longer there.

"You?" cried a person who came out of the shadows of the bookcases, and Claude Lamont stood in the presence of Opal.

Her look was a question, but her lips framed one.

"You've been there?" she cried.

"You sent me down there, didn't you?"

"I did. Well?"

"I always obey you, don't I, sis?"

"You do, Claude. You are my best friend. But tell me—you looked into the room on the right?"

"Yes."

"And——"

"It was empty!"

"Empty? My God!" and Opal, the millionaire's daughter, staggered back and dropped into her father's chair.

CHAPTER XXX.
THE MASTER DETECTIVE'S LITTLE GAME.

"Empty? That house?" again cried Opal, from the depths of the chair. "I cannot believe it."

"It is true. I just came from the place," answered Claude. "What did you do there, sis?"

"I shot him."

"Not the detective?"

"Yes; Carter. I lured him to the place. He was here again, playing his hand. I could not stand it. He was in our way. I wanted him removed. Father was helpless, and the desperate scheme came into my head. I lured him to the Cedar Street house and leaned over the banister, shooting him through the transom while he stood in the parlor."

"And left him there?"

"Yes, yes."

"Well, he wasn't there when I looked into the room." Opal Lamont looked wildly around the library.

"What could have become of him?" she asked.

Claude shook his head.

"Do you think he could not have been dead?"

"I thought you went into the parlor afterward?"

"I did. I bent over him."

"And he appeared at the end of the trail?"

"He did."

"It's a mystery to me."

"Why didn't you look all over the house?"

"That's just what I did."

Opal sat silent for a moment longer, and then she sprang up with a sharp cry.

"If he lives he will try to get even. We must silence this man. It must be done at once."

"Granted. You were a fool to decoy him to the old house."

"I knew of no other place," was the reply. "I took the first plan that entered my head. I never dreamed of failure."

"There, don't think I'm finding fault, sis. You did the best you could; I'm sure of that. The only wonder is that you didn't make a sure shot after what you've done at the galleries."

Half an hour after the interview with his sister Claude Lamont occupied the armchair in the room in which he once showed himself to Carter and Bristol Clara, the latter his near neighbor.

This time he was alone.

Presently he was startled by a rap on the front door, as if some one outside had no use for a bell, and in a moment he had opened it.

He found a well-dressed, dark-faced stranger on the step—a man with a brownish beard and clear, gray eyes.

Claude did not know just what to do with the man, but as he held the door open the fellow entered and faced him in the hall.

"Come this way if you have business with me," said the city sport, and he escorted his caller to the room he had just left.

The man took a chair and laid his hat on his knees.

"To whom am I indebted for this call?" asked Claude.

"Call me Hugh Larkins," answered the stranger, in a squeakish voice that made a sound almost like a file.

"I don't know you, Mr. Larkins."

"Perhaps not. You don't remember me. You have forgotten all about the old place on the Bowery that flourished five or six years ago. You don't recall the barkeeper and the sometime pianist?"

A smile flitted across Claude's face.

"Are you that person?" he asked.

"I'm Hugh Larkins. Sometimes they call me 'Rosy' Larkins, you remember."

"I never recall nicknames."

"Mr. Lamont, you've got good quarters here."

Claude started a little at mention of his name.

"You see, I know you. Why, you haven't changed a great deal. You've got a few more years on you, and you've grown a little stouter—good living, I guess. The 'Daisy Chain' isn't running now, I believe. I dropped into the old place this morning, but the piano stopped four years ago and the hole is a poor bucket shop at present."

"I don't know," said Claude.

"Well, Mr. Lamont, let's to business. I'm a little hard up—somewhat desperate, to make use of a homely phrase."

"And you think I'm a nabob when it comes to cash, eh?"

"I know you're not Lazarus. I've got to have a little chink to keep the proverbial wolf from the door, and——"

"My dear sir, you've struck the wrong place," broke in Claude. "I can't accommodate you."

Larkins fell back in his chair and seemed at his wits' end.

"That's bad," he suddenly squeaked. "It nearly puts me into the river—a desperate man's last resort, you see."

"I can't help that," said Claude coldly. "Every man can do as he pleases with his anatomy, and if you see fit to immerse yours, why, I can't object."

"You can't help Rosy Larkins, who used to play for you at the Daisy Chain? You can't give the old beau a lift?"

"It wouldn't stop with you," was the reply. "It wouldn't stop with you, Rosy."

"I'm but the advance guard, eh?"

"That's it."

Rosy Larkins appeared to get upon his feet with difficulty. He looked down at Claude Lamont and seemed to study him a minute.

"Then I'll have to sell it," said he.

In spite of himself the millionaire's son lost a little color.

"You'll have to sell what?" he asked.

"What I know!"

"See here, that's an old game," cried Claude. "It's a rascal's last resort. You can't blackmail me."

"But I can sell what I know—to the police."

"You don't know anything."

"Do you dare me?"

"Yes."

"All right."

Larkins crossed the room, but stopped at the door, the knob of which he held in his hand.

"You wasn't in the old place that night? Oh, no. You wasn't in Hell's Kitchen a few nights ago? You never go to such a disreputable place? Certainly not. The son of Perry Lamont never goes to such places. Why, of course he doesn't. Hell's Kitchen? Why, there's where Mother Flintstone lived—and died, I believe."

Claude said nothing.

He looked as if his tongue had become riveted to his palate; his eyes seemed to bulge from his head, and his hand dropped from the table at his right.

"Of course you don't go to Hell's Kitchen, because you say you don't," grinned Rosy Larkins in the same squeaky tones.

"What are you driving at?" at last Claude made out to say.

"At just what I've said. I'm pretty plain. My voice isn't as sweet as the notes of the oriole, but you understand my words all the same."

"You certainly don't mean to say that you've got a secret about my going to Hell's Kitchen?"

"Now you've hit it. You wasn't there the night Mother Flintstone was helped out of this world?"

"I was not."

"But I know better."

"You do?"

"Yes; you were there, and Rosy Larkins holds the secret so far all alone."

Claude leaned forward and fastened his gaze upon the face before him.

"Don't you think silence is worth a thousand dollars?" queried his caller.

"Your silence?"

"Mine! That's not a large sum with you who has his hands upon the purse strings of a millionaire. You don't want the police to drag you forward as being connected with the mystery of Hell's Kitchen? I don't want to see one of my old patrons in such a fix."

"Did you see me there?" asked Claude, a little nervously.

"I've got convincing proof."

"But I haven't got the money, Larkins. You will have to come again."

"I won't," said Larkins, and the squeak seemed to get the snarl of a wild beast.

Claude looked at the table and then back at the man.

Larkins was twirling his hat on one of his hands, and his face was still immobile.

"What if I can't raise that amount, and then, what does a man of your present standing want with a thousand dollars?"

"What does a porcupine want with his quills?" flashed the young sport's visitor. "He uses them, that's what. I can use a thousand dollars."

Lamont thought of his own account in bank.

It would not do to give that man a check for the amount, for identification might be followed with unpleasant recollections.

Suddenly he thought of the five thousand he had lately received from Lamont, senior.

A part of it was still in his pocket.

Biting his lips Claude produced the roll of bills and slowly counted out the required amount.

"There, don't come again," he said, looking up at Larkins, whose hand reached out for the money. "But hold on. What assurance have I that you won't sell me out yet?"

"My word."

"If it's no better than your face I'm afraid it's not worth a great deal."

"That's all right. I'm no seraph. Neither was Mother Flintstone, who died that night—you know how," and with this shaft Rosy Larkins opened the door.

As he stepped into the hall his face was for a moment turned from Claude, and that moment the young man whipped a revolver from the table drawer.

As he started up there was a musical click, but the next instant the bare hand of Larkins covered him.

"Don't be a fool," he said. "The secret wouldn't die with me, Mr. Lamont."

The leveled weapon dropped and Claude went back again.

"Aha, good-by. Thanks for the chink. It saves Rosy Larkins from the river," and the man with the squeaky voice was gone.

He went from the scene of the interview almost straight to Mulberry Street; he entered police headquarters and made his way to the superintendent's private office, where he handed the roll of money to a young man.

"Lock it up," said he. "We'll talk about it later. I'm rather tired of this beard," and Carter immediately stood revealed.

CHAPTER XXXI.
IN MOTHER FLINTSTONE'S DEN AGAIN.

The day following these exciting events George Richmond might have been seen bending over a manuscript in a small room some distance from Claude Lamont's apartments.

He had been diligently at work upon the document for some hours, now and then refreshing himself from a bottle on the table.

The chirography was not his own.

It looked for all the world like the writing of an old person taken with the palsy, and the man at work smiled every now and then as he looked at his job.

"It's good for the two hundred thousand," said he, half aloud. "That was a cute bargain Claude made with the old nabob. I am to vanish, of course; but I'll see that I don't lose any of my share. I am to be killed off, and this paper is to fall into Lamont's hands, to be consigned of course to the flames. He'll probably consider it cheap at two hundred thousand, but I'll take care that Claude doesn't really carry out the bargain."

The day had deepened into night, and still George Richmond worked.

He did not stop till the nearest clock struck eight, and then he finished his self-imposed task.

Once more, like a good accountant, he glanced over his pages and stuffed them into an old envelope prepared for the occasion.

"That settles it," he remarked. "Now for the proof of my demise, ha, ha!"

He thrust the whole into his pocket and buttoned his coat over it.

After this he turned the gas low and filled the room with shadows, then pulled his soft hat over his forehead and left the house.

He did not know that he was seen to quit the place.

He was not aware of the fact that during the last part of his work a pair of foxlike eyes were watching him through a rent in the curtain, thanks to a broken slat in the shutter.

The owner of these eyes was on his trail.

It was a boy, shrewd and wiry, and he kept George Richmond in sight, no matter how many turns he made.

Mulberry Billy had not played spy upon this man for nothing.

While he could not see the writing, he felt that it was for no good, and thus he slipped after the man as he crossed one street after another, taking himself into a strange part of New York.

George Richmond visited a well-known cheap café on the Bowery and had a plain supper, after which, once more buttoning his coat to his chin, he sauntered out under the lights.

Billy was still his ferret.

The boy tracked the man to the house occupied at times by Claude Lamont.

He saw him mount the steps, but could not see beyond the door.

George Richmond entered the library and turned on the light.

There he looked around the room, but did not see any one.

Claude was not at home.

Richmond would have started if he could have seen the woman who all the time was closely watching him.

Bristol Clara, Carter's friend, was on the alert, and, having seen him come in, was looking at him through the secret crack.

All at once Richmond started up.

"What a fool I am," he said. "Why didn't I think of it before? I forgot to look under the hearth—the very place an old woman like her would hide precious papers."

He threw a hasty glance toward the door and was about to quit the house when he heard a step.

In another moment Claude Lamont stood before him.

"I've been waiting for you," said Richmond.

"And I've been unavoidably detained. Couldn't get here sooner. Well, have you got the papers?"

Richmond produced his work and threw the bundle upon the table.

Claude pounced upon it and ran over the documents.

"This is good. I didn't know it was in you," he cried, looking up at Richmond.

"I've been trained in more schools than one," was the answer, and Claude looked away.

"Does it suit?" asked Richmond.

"Perfectly."

"Will it deceive the governor?"

"Of course it will. Now you must vanish."

"Yes, I'm to 'die' to his satisfaction. I believe you can't draw any more money till I'm out of the way and the 'confession' in your father's hands."

"That's the bargain."

"Well, I thought of that and dashed off this."

Another bit of paper fell on the table and Claude read:

"FATAL ACCIDENT.

"Last night at ten o'clock a man was seen to fall on the street near the Brussel Block, on Broadway. His companion, apparently frightened by his fall, hastened away, leaving his friend on the pavement. It was discovered that the stricken man was a well-known character named George Richmond, who of late has been subject to attacks of vertigo. The unfortunate man was conveyed from the spot by others who happened to know him, and taken to the rooms of a friend, where he died. Richmond once did time, but of late has not done anything that called for his arrest, though he was known as a shady character, liable to embark on some scheme that promised to add to his wealth, no matter how questionable the transaction."

"That's good!" exclaimed Claude Lamont. "You're dead—as dead as a doornail, and please have the kindness to keep this in view. I don't think you could have done better. Now, what newspaper?"

"I've made the proper arrangements. You can take it to the *Item*. It will cost one hundred to get it inserted, but that's all right. It's dirt cheap."

Claude placed the writing in his pocket and smiled.

"It will hoodwink the old man nicely. He won't want other 'proof.'"

"I thought not."

"I'll see to that. Now I'll attend to the matter. I understand that the item is to appear in but the one paper, and in but one copy at that."

"That's it. Too promiscuous publishing might spoil our plans." The two men arose and left the house.

On the outside the same little figure saw them and again became Carter's spy.

This time Billy tracked Claude Lamont, and saw him enter the office of a morning newspaper with a limited circulation.

He saw him in earnest conversation with a certain attaché of the office, and some money changed hands.

After this Claude Lamont, as Billy found out, seemed quite at ease, for he followed him to a large café, where he ate heartily like a man pleased with what he had done.

Meantime George Richmond had gone to another part of the city.

Once more he entered the locality known in the annals of the police as Hell's Kitchen, and slipped into the room once occupied by Mother Flintstone.

The people who had moved into the place were already gone, a few hours sufficing, and he was alone in the old shell.

Instead of sounding walls and ceiling, as he had done on a former visit, he went straight to the old bricks on the hearth, and commenced lifting them one by one.

To accomplish his purpose the more readily he got down on his knees and worked like a beaver.

Each brick was carefully replaced, and he had gone over half the space when he was interrupted.

A door opened and shut behind him, and George Richmond started to his feet.

A man stood before him.

"There, don't draw," said the person at the door. "It would do you no good, George Richmond. Don't let me disturb you. Go back to your work."

Richmond did not stir.

"Go back to your work, I say. I'll wait till you find it."

"Find what?"

"You know. Your quest."

The ex-convict smiled grimly.

"I was only seeing if the old woman placed anything under the bricks," said he.

"Something valuable, eh?"

"Perhaps."

"Not money, was it, George?"

"Perhaps not."

"You're a cool one. I thought your trip up the river reformed you. Don't you remember how the newspapers exploited your return, and said you were quit of crime? It was a great fake, wasn't it?"

The speaker smiled, but Richmond did not.

"Who are you?" he demanded.

"That's another matter. Don't let me disturb you. You haven't taken up more than half the bricks. Go through the rest."

"I don't care to. You're playing spy, and, by heavens! that's dangerous work."

"You mean that the man who watches you may live to regret it?"

"Yes."

"Well call me spy, then. Don't you think you're playing a pretty bold hand just now, George?"

"I?"

"You. You are into it so deep that you don't want to miss a good thing. There's nothing buried under those bricks; there never was. Mother Flintstone hid it elsewhere."

"That's false. She hid it in this house, and unless you——"

"Come, George, don't show your teeth like a tiger. It will do you no good. You can't find the confession, but the other one will do just as well!"

"What other one?"

It was evident that the question had no sooner left Richmond's lips than he regretted the utterance.

"You know; therefore I need not specify. I hope the work was well done."

"Devil! you've got to fight for your life," and the next instant George Richmond darted forward like a mad beast, and leaping clear of the floor flung himself upon the stranger.

That person braced himself for the ordeal, and warded off the initial blow with the dexterity of a practiced pugilist.

George found himself foiled, but he did not give up.

Again he darted at his enemy, and the pair came together in a deadly grapple.

Back and forth over the floor they writhed like wrestlers before an audience; now George obtaining a little advantage, now the other getting the best of it.

At last Richmond found himself held against the wall by a grip of iron.

He panted in his adversary's power.

"But one man ever held me thus before this," he cried.

"Who was he?"

"Nick Carter, and, by heavens! you must be that same man!"

There was no reply.

CHAPTER XXXII.
MULBERRY BILLY'S "FIND."

Margie Marne came out of the hospital shortly after her terrible experience in the house guarded by Nora.

Her escape had bordered on the miraculous, and the girl was glad to get back to the humble home she occupied.

Her first thought was of the woman who had been her jaileress and she wondered if Nora herself had escaped the flames.

Having a fair acquaintance with Billy, the street Arab, she sought out the boy, and fortunately found him.

Billy had heard of Nora's suicide, and he at once posted Margie.

"By the way," said the little fellow, "I've made a find."

"You? What have you discovered, Billy?"

"Something that I am going to show to Mr. Carter just as soon as I find him."

"It may amount to nothing."

"But you don't know where I found it," cried the boy.

"Tell me."

Billy came closer, and dropped his voice to a whisper as he laid his hand upon the girl's arm.

"I found it in Mother Flintstone's den," said he. "Look here, Margie."

He produced a flat package, which looked like it had been stored away for years, but the moment the girl's eyes alighted on it she uttered a little scream.

"It's the will, Billy!" she exclaimed.

"What had Mother Flintstone to will away, I'd like to know?" said the boy.

"More than you think. Let me see the packet."

Billy laid it on the table, and watched Margie closely.

The girl seemed to be afraid to touch the package, but at last she picked it up.

Opening the envelope, which looked nearly ready to fall to pieces, she drew forth a paper and opened it.

The first line startled her.

"What is it?" asked the boy.

Margie said nothing, but her eyes dilated.

"It's a will, you said, Margie?"

"It's more than that, Billy. It's the true story of Mother Flintstone's life."

"Then it is important, sure enough."

Margie read on, her face changing color, and at last she reached the end of the page.

"Mother Flintstone left behind her an important document," she remarked.

"That's what the dark-faced man was looking for when he sounded the walls."

"No doubt of that."

"P'r'aps that's why they killed her."

"They, Billy? Do you think more than one hand was at work that night?"

"I do, Miss Margie," cried the boy, confidently. "There are two hands in this mystery. Mr. Carter will trip them up in time, see if he don't."

"Yes, Billy, there is more than a will," and Margie held the package up before the street boy. "As I've told you, it is also the story of Mother Flintstone's life. Where did you find it, boy?"

"Under the hearth."

"The place was not examined by the dark-faced man?"

"Exactly! He looked every place else. I found it there safe from him and the rats. Keep it, Margie. No, hide it from that man. He'll have it or your life if he knows you have it."

Margie placed the packet in her bosom, and looked gratefully at the street boy.

"I'll see that you're paid for this find," said she.

"I don't want a penny. I only want ter get ahead of George Richmond and his chum, Claude Lamont, the young sport. They're into the biggest game of their lives, but we'll balk 'em all the same, Margie."

The girl expressed the hope that it would turn out thus, and in a short time she was in another part of the city.

She wanted to avoid the man into whose hands she had fallen at the Trocadero. She was now confident that this personage was Claude Lamont himself, and she had seen enough of his villainy.

Margie Marne carried the precious package home, where she hid it carefully, believing that no human eye could find it, and was satisfied.

Night was coming on, and she quitted her humble lodgings, with her hood pulled over her face so as to hide it.

She had a visit to make, and soon she reached the room occupied by Carter.

Her raps were not answered, and she looked disappointed.

When she again reached the street the lamps had been lit, and the girl looked all about her.

Thinking of the package she started home, but on a corner not far from Carter's rooms a hand fell upon her arm.

Margie started, and uttered a little cry. She looked around at the same time and into the face of a man, who leered at her with a half-vicious look.

"Don't fly so fast, my bird," laughed the fellow. "I don't intend to soil your plumage. You're Miss Margie Marne, aren't you?"

"What if I am?"

"Then you're the very person I want to see."

"But I don't want to see any one."

"I suppose not. That's the way with some girls. I'm Caddy."

"Who's Caddy?" demanded Margie.

"I'm the 'mixer' at the Trocadero."

The mention of that name sent a chill through the girl's nerves, and she fell back.

"Don't mention that horrid place!" she exclaimed.

"I know you had a rather unpleasant experience there, but, you see, it wasn't my fault. I can tell you something that may give you a chance to get even."

"Speak quick, if you can. What is it?"

"Let's drop in here," and the little man pointed toward a decent-looking restaurant.

Eager to learn something more about the man who had decoyed her to the Trocadero, Margie went with the fellow, and he guided her to a little table in the darkest corner of the place.

"Why don't you bleed him?" were the first words when they had seated themselves.

"Is that your suggestion? Do you want to make a blackmailer out of me?" exclaimed the girl.

"No; it wouldn't be blackmail in this case," explained Caddy. "It would simply be getting pay for the indignity."

"I'll get even with him some other way," said Margie. "You know him, do you?"

"Why, of course. Ha, ha, nobody comes to the Trocadero whom I don't catch on to. Beat Caddy out of the game, if you can! You don't want to make him pay the fiddler, then?"

"Not in the manner you've suggested."

"You're a fool!" cried the little man. "See here, I'll help you all I can. I'll go halves with you, and you won't have to take any risk. He'll milk."

"But I'm not in that business."

Caddy at once changed color.

His round face became positively hideous.

He leaned across the table like a thoroughbred villain and his teeth seemed to snap together.

"If you don't bleed him you'll get into the net again," he suddenly cried.

"Which means, I suppose, that you'll help get me there?"

"I didn't say I would, but I won't help keep you out."

Margie flushed.

"You miserable wretch, keep your distance!" she exclaimed, and would have left the table but for the clutch of the little man's hand.

"When you can't cajole you threaten. It won't pay, sir."

"I'll see that it does pay!" laughed the mixer of the Trocadero, unabashed. "I know my business. Sit down."

Margie was thrust back into her chair, and the fellow leered at her again.

"If you don't want to milk the young sport himself, bleed the old man. He's a bird with golden plumage."

"What's his name?"

"Gad, don't you know? It's Perry Lamont. Lives on one of the avenues and has mints of wealth at his command. He's a pigeon worth plucking, girl."

"No, let others do that."

"Where did you get your scruples, I'd like to know?" sneered Caddy. "You're one in ten thousand. Why, you can feather your nest in fine shape——"

Margie broke loose from the fellow's grasp and fell back.

He arose at the same time and came around the table.

"Don't touch me, serpent!" cried the girl. "You can't use me in any of your schemes. I try to be honest."

"You do, eh? Oh, you'll get over it in time. Get a few more years on you and you'll be as tough——"

"Here, what's that? That's an honest girl, sir," put in a man eating quietly at another table. "Don't touch her, you little sinner, or I'll break your neck."

The speaker arose and came forward, gazed at by Caddy with feelings of fear, while Margie thanked him mutely for his interference.

"I don't know you, miss, but I've seen this man," continued the stranger, who was tall and broad-shouldered. "I guess it's not the first time for him. Get out."

He pushed Caddy down the aisle with his large hand, and the little drink mixer went without much urging.

"I'll see you later!" he flashed at Margie.

"No threats!" cried the other man. "Get out, I say, and the sooner the better."

Then the tall man turned to Margie and said:

"Pardon me, but I thought I heard him call you Margie. It cannot be Miss Margie Marne whom I address?"

"That's my full name, sir," said the girl, dropping her eyes.

"My name is McDonald—Jerry McDonald. I own a little business property in this city. The man who just left is a little rascal. I suppose he decoyed you hither?"

Margie told the story of her coming to the place, and McDonald said:

"He's revengeful, and you will do well to look after him. If you ever need my assistance in any way don't hesitate to command it," and he handed the girl his card.

In another moment the still astonished girl was alone.

CHAPTER XXXIII.
THE COST OF A SECRET.

George Richmond found himself suddenly free from his antagonist in Mother Flintstone's den.

The battle ended sooner than he thought, for his enemy gave a lurch which disengaged them, and when George recovered he was the sole occupant of the place.

"Who was he?" the astonished man asked himself.

The reply came from his imagination, and he sprang to the door and looked out.

No one there.

"I accused him of being Carter, the detective, but he did not reply," he went on. "Years ago I was in Carter's hands and the grip to-night seemed the same. But I may have been mistaken. I mustn't forget that years have passed since Carter caught me red-handed. I cannot believe that my foe to-night was the detective."

George did not resume his inspection of the old hearth, for he turned away after replacing the last brick and slipped into the street.

He was to vanish now.

That was his bargain with Claude Lamont, and he knew that the fictitious account of his death was even then in the hands of the printers.

He turned up later in another part of the city.

He crossed the bridge and vanished in Brooklyn.

Chuckling to himself, he thought of how he had played it on Perry Lamont.

In a small room he threw himself upon a couch to snatch a little sleep.

He was to be pronounced dead by the newspaper to Perry Lamont.

That was a part of the conspiracy.

Claude, the blackmailer of his own father, was to attend to that part of the work and he—George—was to get some of the blood money.

Thinking how easily the game moved onward to success, he fell asleep, nor waked till the next morning.

Then he set about disguising himself most thoroughly.

He changed his eyebrows, he darkened his hair and he gave his upper lip a sweeping mustache.

After his work no one would have called him George Richmond.

Meantime, over in the larger city, Perry Lamont, entering the library earlier than usual, as if he expected to hear some news, found Claude there.

Father and son looked at one another for a second, and Claude pointed at a newspaper on the desk.

The millionaire picked it up and his eager eyes discerned a pencil mark at a certain paragraph.

He devoured the falsehood eagerly and almost out of breath.

The young sport watched him like a cat.

"Thank Heaven!" cried Perry Lamont, as he shot a glance at Claude and dropped into his chair.

"It suits you, I see."

"Suits me?" was the reply. "You know it does."

A momentary silence followed between father and son, and then the elder Lamont said:

"Did you have any trouble?"

"Not much."

"Did he suspect you?"

"Yes, he did that; but I had to go on, you know."

"I know. He died for sure?"

It was a singular question, as if the speaker half suspected the truth, and Claude's heart seemed to find a lodgment in his throat.

"What does the paper say?" cried Claude, a little irritated. "It records the death of the notorious George Richmond, doesn't it?"

"It does."

"That's sufficient, I think. Do you want to see the—body?"

"My God, no!"

"Nor the burial certificate? They'll probably hold a post mortem, but we're safe all the same. It's all right, I assure you. There's no danger, but it took work."

"I'm proud of you, Claude. Now, what about the papers?"

"I've got them, too."

"Here?"

"Yes," and Claude dived one hand into an inner pocket and drew forth a package, at sight of which Lamont's eyes seemed to bulge from his head.

"There they are," he resumed, throwing the packet upon the table.

The millionaire snatched at it and opened the package.

He found the documents forged by George Richmond, and opened the first one.

"Heavens! what have we escaped?" he ejaculated. "It was a very narrow escape. Did you read these papers, Claude?"

"No, never thought of that. I don't care to know what the old hag was."

"Great Cæsar! these papers would have destroyed us," and Perry Lamont looked white. "She had it in her power to break me up, and I don't see why she didn't exercise it. Why, they're worth a million almost."

For some time Perry Lamont went over the papers in silence and did not look up again till he had reached the end of the last sheet.

Claude smiled inwardly all the time.

He knew that George had done his work well.

"Now, here they go," said Lamont, senior, at last, as he moved toward the grate where a fire burned.

Claude saw his father hold the documents over the fire a few moments and then drop them into it.

As they caught fire the door opened and Opal came in.

Her face was white and she was agitated.

Perry Lamont pointed in silence at the hearth and looked toward his daughter.

Opal sprang to the fire and bent forward.

"Did you get it?" she asked, looking at her brother.

Claude said nothing.

"Did you have any trouble?"

"Some."

"You paid him well for that service, didn't you?" she inquired of her father.

"We had an understanding."

"That's good. It saved us. We are no longer in the toils of the secret-keeper. Now no one can say that Mother Flintstone was our near kin."

The tall, regal-looking girl seemed almost beside herself with joy.

She would have embraced Claude had not his coldness repulsed her, and in a few moments she withdrew.

"I'll take it now," said Claude, addressing his parent.

"Oh, yes. You'll place it to your account, I suppose?"

"Of course."

Perry Lamont filled out a check for two hundred thousand dollars, and pushed it across the desk to his son.

Claude looked at it a moment, and then transferred it to his pocket.

It was the cost of a secret; it was also blood money, and the time was near at hand when that deed was to return to plague the doers.

"Safe at last!" exclaimed Perry Lamont, when he found himself alone. "It's in the fire and he's out of the way. I would like to know if Claude really had much trouble. The paper said it was vertigo, but we know better. Claude is sure the post mortem will not reveal anything. They won't catch Claude!"

He chuckled to himself and looked at the darkened ashes of the false confession in the grate.

By and by he returned to the desk and sat down, his head falling on his breast like that of a weary man, and in a short time he was fast asleep.

The house grew still. Outside Claude Lamont was hurrying downtown, while Opal, in the parlor almost for the first time since her bout with the detective, thrummed the piano.

Some distance from the Lamont mansion Carter, the detective, was watching the actions of a man who mixed drinks behind a bar.

It was Caddy, the mixer at the Trocadero, and the detective, well disguised, seemed to take more than a passing interest in his movements.

By and by Caddy put on his coat and walked out, with Carter at his heels.

All at once the hand of the detective fell upon Caddy's shoulder, and the little man stopped at once.

His face grew white when he looked up and saw the keen eyes that seemed to read his inmost thoughts.

"Don't do it again," said the detective.

"What have I done?"

"Don't threaten Miss Marne again."

"But I—I—didn't."

"You did. Please don't try it any more. That's all."

Caddy did not catch his breath till Carter was out of sight, and even then he seemed to breathe hard.

"Won't I?" he hissed. "Just let me get another chance at the girl, and I'll make her think she isn't anybody in particular. She refused to play her part of the game I've made up, but I'll bring her around in spite of the two men, that I will."

But for all his braggadocio Caddy was ill at ease, for instead of going on he retraced his steps to the Trocadero, took a "bracer," and remained indoors.

Nick Carter proceeded on his way, and at last pulled up in front of Bristol Clara's house.

The woman opened the door even before he knocked and led him into the parlor.

"George Richmond is dead," she exclaimed, a smile coming to her lips. "Not quite dead, but I heard the arrangements made. It's a cool scheme, isn't it? Who are they going to beat out of two hundred thousand dollars?"

"Perry Lamont, the millionaire," was the answer. "They're all birds of the same feather, even the girl. I had a narrow escape from her, but a miss is just as good as a mile. She may know ere this that I don't lie dead in the parlor of the old mansion on Cedar Street. I want a place at the peephole to-night, Clara."

"It's at your service."

"I won't need it after to-night."

"Are you going to close in on them?"

The detective nodded.

"Which one did it?" eagerly asked the girl.

"Never mind, Clara. I won't make any mistake."

"Of course not. You never do," proudly answered the tenant of the house.

Carter had set his time, but he could not prophesy what the coming hours were to bring forth.

CHAPTER XXXIV.
BETWEEN THE WALLS OF DOOM.

Shrewd as the detective was, he was destined to meet one who was almost his equal in dexterity and cunning before the hour set for closing in on his quarry came around.

When he quitted Bristol Clara's abode he proceeded to his own quarters, where he desired, for the time, to be alone.

The secrets of the trail he kept to himself.

If he knew the hand which struck Mother Flintstone down he did not reveal it by word or deed, and, like the experienced tracker, he was silent.

Several hours later the detective left the rooms and reappeared on the street.

He was within a block of his place when a boy approached him.

He extended a letter, which the detective at once took.

"Who sent this, boy?" he asked, as he glanced at the superscription.

"The leddy, sir."

"But who was the lady?"

"Look inside. I guess that tells; ha, ha!" and the messenger whisked around the nearest corner and disappeared.

Already the hands of Carter had broken the seal of the missive thus strangely delivered, and in a moment he had read:

"Could you spare me five minutes of your valuable time, Mr. Carter? I can make some dark places clear to you. I can enlighten you about some important things. Come secretly, for it is ticklish business. I will be there. Come to Number — Hester Street. Don't knock! just open the door and come to the first room on the left of the hall.

"Sara P——"

Nick Carter read the letter twice before he looked up again.

He did not know Sara P——.

He had never heard of such a person, and he racked his brain in vain to think who she might be.

He did not know what "dark places" she referred to.

She might mean some old trail which he had run down, or she might have reference to Mother Flintstone's taking off.

The detective was puzzled.

However, he decided to see if there was anything in the affair, to go to the designated number and meet this woman-informer face to face.

As no time was set by the strange writer, he took it for granted that she was to be found in the house at any hour, and in a few minutes he was on his way.

The detective was always ready to investigate anything that promised to assist him on a trail.

More than once he had picked up some startling clews from anonymous letters, and he thought that perhaps "Sara P———" might know something of importance.

Hester Street is not the finest street in Gotham. Neither is it a high-toned thoroughfare. There is a mixture of poverty and wealth on Hester Street, but society there in spots is not of the highest order.

Carter entered the street with some misgivings, but not afraid.

He walked leisurely up the street, looking for the number, and wondering what sort of looking woman his correspondent was.

He found the house at last—a plain, two-story affair, with shutters in front and signs of age about the structure.

No one appeared at the door to greet him, but he did not expect any one.

He walked up the steps and turned the knob.

The door opened easily, and he was in the hall.

"The first door to the left," he mentally said, and then he advanced toward it.

In another second he had pushed this portal open and stood in a darkened room.

He saw no one.

Perhaps "Sara P———" was in another part of the house and had not heard him enter.

Suddenly, however, he was undeceived, and in a flash he knew he had entered another trap.

The floor gave way beneath his feet, as if his weight had suddenly broken it in.

The entire floor seemed to fall.

The detective made an effort to recover his equilibrium, but the Fates were against him.

He fell down—down—and struck on his feet to pitch forward in Stygian darkness.

At the same time a strange noise overhead told him that the floor had resumed its original position, and then for a few moments all was still.

The trapped detective had to smile to himself in spite of his surroundings.

He could not help laughing at his situation, however dark and hopeless it seemed to be; he had been cleverly caught, and the bait had secured the prize.

It did not take him long to recover from the fall, which had not injured him; only jarred him up a little.

He went forward and found a wall ahead.

He followed the wall around, and came back to the same spot, as he could tell by a little stone under his feet.

The dungeon apparently had no outlet; it was like a sealed-up prison of the olden time.

Carter put up his hands, but could not touch the floor overhead.

Of course he could not tell how far he had fallen, but he knew that the trap was directly above him.

Had "Sara P——" sprung the trap?

Had she lured him to this place to destroy him, and thus get even for some of his detective work?

He did not doubt it.

Nick Carter, in the underground prison, said nothing while he went around the walls.

He heard no noises in the house overhead, and no one seemed to walk the floors there.

At last the detective struck a match on the stone wall.

It revealed the dimensions of the dungeon, and he surveyed it with eager curiosity. It was a dungeon sure enough. He saw the stone walls and the manner in which the stones were put together. There was no escape.

Holding the little light above his head Carter saw the underpinning of the floor.

He also found the strong iron hinges upon which the great trap had worked at crime's bidding.

He was like a trapped fox.

Hemmed in by walls of stone, with an impregnable ceiling overhead, where could there be an avenue of escape?

All at once, at the last flashing of the lucifer, the detective saw some words on the wall.

It reminded him of the words on the wall of the room where Jack, his spy, had been strangled.

Had the same hand written them there?

He threw the match to the ground, struck another and sprang eagerly forward.

He held the little light against the wall and read as follows:

"I am doomed to perish here. There is no escape from this hole of death. I was decoyed here like a rabbit, and I die for my folly. Let the next unfortunate person know that I, Lewis Newell, was the victim of Opal Lamont's cunning. The woman is a tigress. Farewell.

"LEWIS NEWELL."

For a full half minute the detective seemed to hold his breath.

He read the writing again and again, and at last threw the stump of the match at his feet.

Doomed to die!

Another had been before him, and that person ascribed his end to Opal Lamont.

Was this accusation true?

The old detective recalled his adventure in the house on Cedar Street and how narrowly he had escaped death at the hands of this same girl.

Perhaps this house belonged to the millionaire, like that one.

Once more in darkness, Carter had time to study the situation.

His curiosity got the better of him, and again he looked at the writing on the wall.

It looked plainer than ever now.

Who was Lewis Newell, the former victim?

He had never heard of such a person, but he did not doubt the truth of the inscription.

Suddenly the detective heard a sound that seemed to come from above.

As he turned his face upward the floor seemed to lift, and his eyes were blinded by an intense glare.

It was as if an electric globe had suddenly been uncovered in his face, and the light was so strong that he fell back, blinking his eyes like an owl.

The glare vanished as suddenly as it came into being, but when he looked again he caught sight of a little ball burning in one corner of the trap.

It sent out a singular odor, not unpleasant, but enervating, and the detective's system seemed to yield to its influence from the first.

"The accursed thing is the death agent which may have killed Newell!" he cried, as he sprang forward and set his foot on the burning ball.

At that moment an explosion occurred, the interior of the dungeon seemed to collapse and Carter became unconscious.

Perhaps the end had come.

When the detective came out of the darkness of doom, as it were, he was lying on his face.

In a moment he staggered up and put out his hands.

They touched a wall as hard and cold as the one they had touched last.

Where was he and in what sort of trap?

Slowly the adventures of the last few hours came back to his excited brain.

He recalled the note, the visit to the house on Hester Street, the fall through the trapdoor and the burning ball.

These thoughts came fast and thick; they seemed to contend for supremacy in his brain and he breathed hard.

"I must get out," was his cry. "Woman or tigress, she shall not keep me in this vile place!"

But getting out was the puzzle.

He circumnavigated his prison like a captive in the dungeons of Venice.

He sounded every foot of space, stood on his tiptoes in a vain effort to reach the ceiling, felt the walls again and again and at last gave up.

For once at least the famous detective seemed at the end of life.

CHAPTER XXXV.
A COMPLETE KNOCK-OUT.

Meanwhile, Margie Marne was having an adventure of her own, to which we will now recur.

In another part of the city, and about the same hour that witnessed the strange explosion in the dungeon where Carter was confined, the girl sat in her little room.

She was quite alone, but all the time she was watched by a pair of eyes that did not lose sight of her.

These eyes glittered in the head of a man on the floor above, and he was enabled to watch the girl through a hole deftly cut in the floor.

All unconscious of the espionage, the girl looked over a few papers which she had taken from their hiding place in one corner of the room, where they would baffle the lynx eyes of a keen man, and now and then a smile came to her face.

All at once she heard footsteps approach her door, and for the first time in an hour she looked up.

A rap sounded, but Margie hesitated.

Should she open the door and admit her visitor?

Perhaps it was Carter, whom she wanted to see just then, but a sudden fear took possession of her.

At last, however, Margie arose, and hiding the papers in her bosom, crossed the room.

Her hand was on the latch, but for all this she still hesitated.

In another moment, as if beating down her last suspicion, Margie opened the door.

A man stood before her. It was not the person who had offered to protect her from Caddy's advances, nor was it Caddy himself.

As she held the door open the stranger advanced into the apartment and turned suddenly upon Margie.

Her breath went fast, and she gazed at the man with half-stifled feelings.

"Miss Marne?" he asked in a peculiar voice.

"Yes, sir."

"Alone, I see."

"I am quite alone, but I cannot imagine to whom I owe the present call."

"Sit down, girl."

There was something commanding in the tones, which had suddenly changed, but Margie did not stir.

"I want to talk with you," continued the man. "And I prefer to have you seated."

Margie glanced at the door and then toward the window, the eyes of her caller following her, and for half a second her heart seemed in her throat.

"I want those papers," and the fellow, whose face was covered with a heavy brown beard, held out his hand.

"What papers?" demanded the girl.

"The ones you have just been looking over."

No wonder Margie started.

"Come, don't mince matters with me. I won't have it. Are they in your bosom, girl?"

Margie fell back, but the man advanced.

"I am here for them," he went on. "You can't cheat me out of them. Come, hand them over."

"But——"

"Not a word unless you intend to comply with my demand! You know where the papers are. You got them in Mother Flintstone's den."

"My God——"

"I hit the nail on the head, did I?" brutally laughed the man. "I thought my arrow wouldn't go far wide of the mark. Here, I'll despoil you of the papers by force if you don't tamely submit."

Margie was nearly against the wall now, and she looked at the man like a startled fawn.

She now felt, yes, knew that the beard was but a mask, and she asked herself whom she faced.

Claude Lamont or George Richmond?

She could retreat no farther, and remembering her adventure in the house which had succumbed to the fire fiend, she nearly fainted.

Already the powerful hands of the unknown almost touched her bosom; she could feel his hot, wine-laden breath on her cheek and she expected any minute to be hurled across the room and robbed.

She made one last effort, but the movement was intercepted, and she stood in his grasp!

He held her at arms' length and glared at her after the manner of a wild beast.

The poor girl was a child in the iron grip of the man, and all at once he drew her toward him and began to look for the documents.

"Don't! For Heaven's sake, have some respect for my sex!" gasped Margie. "You can have them."

"I can, eh? Well, hand them over."

Margie, with trembling fingers, did so, and at sight of the papers he uttered a gleeful cry.

The next moment he released her, and she sank into the nearest chair.

She saw him step back a pace and open the papers, over which he eagerly ran his eye.

"Is this all you had, girl?" he suddenly demanded.

"Yes."

"It's a lie!"

Margie's face colored.

"I want the others."

"I have no others."

"These are but letters from a lover. Where are the papers that once belonged to the old hag?"

"That is not for me to tell."

"You defy me, eh?"

"I defy no one."

"I'll choke you to death but what I get the truth. I'll have the right papers or your life!"

"You must take my life, then."

The girl had strangely recovered her self-possession.

She could look at him now without flinching, and the terrible hand dreaded a few moments before had no terrors for her now.

Suddenly the man threw the letters upon the table and looked fiercely at the girl.

She withstood his look like a heroine.

"Be quick about it!" he cried.

"I have no other papers," calmly said Margie.

He laughed derisively and then glanced toward the door.

"I'll fix you," he exclaimed. "You've been in our road long enough, and the only sure way to get rid of you is to leave you here a fit subject for the morgue."

The moment he came toward her Margie sprang up.

She was strong again, and suddenly catching up a poker which stood near the chair, she placed herself in an attitude of defiance.

"You advance at your peril," she said, in determined tones. "I shall defend myself to the last extremity."

"Against me? Why, girl, you don't know what you are saying."

"You shall find out if you advance, I say."

He laughed again, and came forward.

In an instant the heavy rod was lifted above the girl's head, and the next second she brought it down with all her might.

It was a blow such as a giantess might have delivered, for the man's lifted arms went down, and he received the full weight of the poker upon his head.

He gave one gasp and sank to the floor like one killed outright, and Margie, with the novel weapon still clutched in her hands, looked at him, while a deathly pallor overspread her face.

Had she killed him?

For a short time she stood there, barely realizing that the whole thing was not a dream, and then she bent over the man.

As she touched the beard it came off and fell to the floor beside the face.

Margie uttered a scream.

She had seen that face before—seen it in company with Claude Lamont, and she knew that the man was his associate in evil and one of the chief men in the plot against Mother Flintstone and herself.

She sprang up suddenly and ran from the room, shutting the door behind her.

Down on the street she saw no one, though she looked everywhere for a policeman.

Moments were flitting away, and she suddenly thought of Carter.

She knew where he lodged, and she would tell him of her adventure.

In a moment she was on her way, but she was doomed to disappointment; the detective's door was locked and she could not elicit a response.

Baffled, Margie turned back again.

She had taken up nearly twenty minutes on the streets, and when she reached the vicinity of her humble home she thought of the man left on the floor.

She glided upstairs cautiously, just as if the dead could hear her, but at the door she stopped and listened.

All was still beyond it.

Margie put on a bold front, and opened the portal.

The first look seemed to root her to the spot.

The room was untenanted.

No one lay on the floor, and the little place, with this exception, seemed just as she left it.

The man, her victim, was gone.

"Thank Heaven! his blood is not on my hands, rascal though he was!" exclaimed Margie Marne, as she leaped across the threshold and shut the door behind her.

If she had returned a little sooner she might have caught sight of her would-be robber.

She might have seen a man come out of the house, with his hat drawn over his brows and the brown beard awry.

This individual hurried away, nor looked he back, as if he thought he was not safe from molestation, and his gait told how eager he was to get out of the neighborhood.

A few minutes later he turned up in a certain house in another part of the city, and dropped into a chair as the tenant of the room demanded to know if he had been in a prize fight.

"Not quite, but I struck an Amazon," was the reply, and he of the brown beard tried to smile.

"Tell me; did you encounter Margie?"

"No one else. What made you guess her?"

"Her name popped into my head somehow or other. Guess I must have been thinking of her when you came in. What did she hit you with?"

"With a crowbar, from the way my head feels; but never mind. It's a long lane, you know."

Claude Lamont smiled.

"You do pretty well for a 'dead man,'" and then both men burst into a laugh.

"I'll wring her neck for it yet!" suddenly cried George Richmond. "I'll have the blood of that girl for her blow!"

CHAPTER XXXVI.
THE PARRICIDE.

"You'd better not try it."

"Why not?" snarled Richmond.

"She may be dangerous."

"That chit? Pshaw!"

"Just try it. See here. You don't want to be too gay just now. Don't you know you're a dead man?"

"So I am."

"Well, be a little careful. What if Carter gets on to our game?"

"Carter mustn't do that."

"Of course not, but we must see that he cannot."

Ten minutes longer the two men, watched by Bristol Clara, the tenant in the next house, remained in the room, and then Richmond bade Claude good night.

The moment the millionaire's son found himself alone he struck the table with his fist.

"Why didn't I really kill that man?" he exclaimed. "He is bound to be my evil genius, after all. I can't see my way clear to ultimate success with him in the way. He'll blackmail me, and what can I do? If he were really dead——"

He did not finish the sentence, but broke it off suddenly, and arose, throwing his cigar away.

"I'll go home," he said.

A few minutes later he was met at the door of his home by his sister Opal, whose face told him that she had something of importance to say.

"Father is gone," said the girl, with a gasp, and would have fallen if Claude had not caught her around the waist.

"Gone?" echoed the young sport.

"It is true. You can see for yourself."

Opal led the way to the library, and mutely pointed at her father's chair.

"When did you miss him?" asked Claude.

"An hour ago."

"Did he leave any message behind?"

"Yes."

"Where is it?"

Opal handed her brother a crumpled note, and the young man leaned toward the light to read its contents.

"My God! you don't believe that?" he exclaimed, turning upon his sister.

"I don't know what to believe," was the answer.

"What have you done?"

"Nothing. I've been waiting for you. I sent to the club, but the message came back that you had not been there."

"Something must be done. Certainly father did not mean this. He has not gone to the police."

"I—don't—know."

"I'll see. He may have gone to the river in a fit of madness. He would not tell all he knows about Mother Flintstone."

"I should think he would not."

Claude seized his hat and rushed from the house.

For a little while his brain seemed to swim, and the lights blinded him.

He did not ask what Opal would do now that she was again the sole occupant of the house.

He did not seem to care.

Perry Lamont was a runaway, with a great secret at his tongue's end and millions at stake.

For some time the old nabob had been subject to strange spells of mania, and the worst was to be feared.

It was this that urged Claude Lamont on and on.

He could not wait till he got downtown, and minutes seemed hours to him.

He thought of a thousand things.

He wondered what had become of Carter, and more than once he looked back, as if he expected to see Nick on his trail.

At a fashionable saloon he stopped long enough to gulp down something for his nerves, and then he hastened on again.

Suddenly he stopped, and then dropped into the shadow of a large building.

A man was crossing the street—coming toward him.

His heart took a great leap into his throat, for it was the very man he was hunting for—his father.

Claude stood in the shadows and watched him like a hawk.

He could not take his eyes off the old man, and as he neared him he debated in his mind what to do.

As the millionaire stepped upon the sidewalk within a few feet of him the son darted forward and clutched him by the arm.

"Father!" he cried.

With a powerful effort Perry Lamont shook the grip loose and looked into Claude's face.

"My God! he's mad!" ejaculated the young man.

"It is Claude. Don't you know me?" pleaded the son.

"Let me go. I've been looking after my sister—little Sis, you know."

"Heavens! he means Mother Flintstone!" thought Claude.

"I can't find her. What's become of Sis?"

"I'll find her for you."

"What; you'll show me where she is?" cried the old man.

"Yes, yes. Come with me."

In an instant Lamont's mind changed, and he became as docile as a lamb.

As Claude was near the house he occupied when not at home he guided his father thither and let him inside.

Conducting him to the library, where he had just had an interview with George Richmond, he seated his parent and took a chair himself.

"Is she here?" asked Lamont.

"Yes; you'll see her presently."

"But I can't wait. I want to see Sis now. I haven't seen her for years, and I want to tell her about the money I have kept for her so long."

"What money?"

"I've kept it for Sis. It belongs to her—the thousands which were left to her, you know."

"What if Sis isn't in need of money?" queried Claude.

"Then I'll throw it into the fire! No one shall have it but her. I will see to that. Who are you?"

Claude smiled grimly.

His father had not recognized him.

"Come, you don't want Sis to have the money," he cried, and before the son could prevent, the other was on his feet, his eyes glaring like the orbs of a wolf.

"I'll have your blood if you don't tell me!" shrieked the mad millionaire.

"I'm your son."

"No, you're not! My son? It's a lie!"

Claude saw his danger, and the madman advancing upon him made him throw out his hand in self-defense.

"My son is at home!" cried Lamont, senior. "You are not he. I won't believe it!"

"But, father——"

The sentence was not finished, for all at once Perry Lamont sprang at his son, and grabbing him by the shoulders, threw him against the wall.

There was a startled cry on the other side of it from the woman whose eyes seemed glued to the paper there.

"I'll kill you like a dog if you don't tell me where Sis is. I went to her den—they called her Mother Flintstone, you know—but she wasn't there. Where is she?"

"Let me loose first."

"And let you run off? Not much; ha! ha!" and the maniac laughed. "I won't do anything of the kind."

"But I can't show you where Sis is unless you do that. I won't run away, father."

"It is false. You can't fool me. I will hold you here till you tell the truth."

"Well, Sis, is asleep in the room yonder."

"Is that true?"

Claude Lamont wanted to gain time. If he could get rid of his father's maddened hands he might effect his escape, for just now he was in danger.

Perry Lamont glanced toward the door, and seemed disposed to believe his desperate son.

But suddenly he appeared to change his mind, for again his eyes shot forth sparks of fire.

"Call her out here," he said.

Claude's heart seemed to sink within him.

He knew he could not call back the dead.

He wished for the door to open and admit some one; he would have rejoiced then, with his father's fingers buried in his throat, to have seen Carter.

"I'll give you one second, or to hades you go!" suddenly cried Perry Lamont.

Claude's blood seemed to run cold.

One second to live!

What had become of George Richmond?

Why didn't that worthy turn up to save him in the nick of time?

Why had he guided his father to that house and not home, where he would have had Opal for an ally?

Fate was against him.

"Quick! quick!" exclaimed the madman. "Tell me where Sis is or I will tear your throat here!"

Claude made one last effort.

He summoned all his strength and dashed forward.

His father's feet tripped on the carpet, and, falling, he dragged him down.

Father and son fell in a heap on the carpet, and for half a second seemed stunned by the tumble.

Claude was the first to recover.

He raised himself and tore himself loose from the maniacal fingers.

As he did so his father sprang up with the roar of a baffled tiger, and launched himself forward.

It left Claude little time for reflection or action.

He saw danger ahead, and his hands were bare of any weapon.

But suddenly he snatched up a glass paper weight from the desk, and launched it straight at his father's face.

An arrow never went straighter to the mark than did the paper weight. It struck the millionaire fairly in the face, and he went down like a stricken ox.

On the carpet he gave a convulsive gasp and moved one arm; that was all.

"He invited it," said Claude. "He forced it upon himself. They can't blame me for this thing."

Five minutes later he stood on the street, with the house darkened behind him and the glim of the lamps in his eyes.

He looked like Cain; the brand was on his brow.

CHAPTER XXXVII.
CARTER'S ESCAPE.

We left Carter in durance in the dungeon where the strange explosion had taken place.

Truly the detective was in the direst straits, and he could not forget the writing on the wall.

He did not know who "Lewis Newell" was, and he did not stop to inquire.

The sentence said that Opal Lamont, the fair daughter of the millionaire, was responsible for the prisoner's fate, and this set the detective to thinking.

Perhaps the house to which he had been decoyed belonged to Perry Lamont, like another house he knew of.

He recalled his visit to the nabob's mansion, where he had confronted Opal, and he recalled as well her demeanor.

That she had revengeful blood he well knew.

Her beauty was tigerish.

But first of all the detective wanted to get out of the dark place, and he resolved that it should not hold him long.

How to get out was the question, but for all this he set about it with all his wits at work.

The singular odors arising from the bomb had not overcome him longer than a few minutes, and now the dungeon seemed fairly free of them.

Once more he went around the walls and sounded them again. He stooped where he had seen the flash of light as the bomb burst, and found that the wall had yielded.

A stone was loosened, and this gave him hope.

Beyond the wall must lie liberty.

With an energy born of despair Carter toiled until he had made a hole underneath the wall large enough to admit his body, and he did not hesitate to squeeze through it.

Beyond the wall sure enough lay freedom, for he felt the cool night air on his cheeks and found himself in a cramped back yard.

Out of durance at last, Carter breathed a prayer of thankfulness and filled up the hole.

He stood for some little time in the yard, and then cleared the fence which stood between him and the street.

Half an hour later he might have been seen to enter Bristol Clara's house.

The woman uttered a cry as she saw him, and pulled him forward.

"Thank Heaven!" she cried; "but why didn't you come sooner?"

"I couldn't. Circumstances prevented," said the detective, with a grim smile, which Bristol Clara did not understand.

"What's happened, girl?"

"Murder!"

"Where?"

"There!"

The woman pointed across the room toward the next house and looked at Carter.

"Who committed it?" he asked.

"Claude Lamont."

"Then they're even," was the detective's answer.

Clara did not reply, but led the detective to the peephole, and bade him look.

The room beyond the partition was dimly lighted, but he could see its appointments and single tenant.

A man was stretched on the floor, silent and still.

"That's the victim," said the woman at his side.

"Who is he?"

"Perry Lamont."

"And you say Claude did it? His son?"

"His son. I saw the whole affair."

"Tell me all about it, Clara."

Bristol Clara did so, and the detective listened without once interrupting the woman.

"I must see the man yonder," said Nick.

"That's easy. The house is tenanted only by the dead. You can easily get inside."

It did not take Carter long to reach the room where Perry Lamont lay.

He raised the man's head and saw the dark spot made by the murderous paper weight; then he lowered it again to the floor.

He searched the room thoroughly, and found more than one thing which told him that it had been one of Claude Lamont's nests.

At last he rejoined Clara in the other house.

"Now for the round-up," said he.

The woman looked at him, but did not speak.

"You once asked me who killed Mother Flintstone," said Nick.

"Yes."

"I know."

"Of course you do. You find out all these things. I never doubted that you would reach the end of this trail."

"Well, woman, I can tell you now."

Bristol Clara leaned forward, and Carter whispered a word into her ear.

"My God! you don't mean that?" cried the woman, as she recoiled, with very little color in her face.

"Every word of it."

"It cannot be."

"It is true."

"Then go and do your duty;" said she. "Don't let the guilty escape, Mr. Carter."

"I don't intend to. I'll see you later, Clara. Only keep a watch over the man in yonder. The murderer may come back. Perhaps it was self-defense, but he isn't remorseful. It is murder all the same."

The detective made his way from the house and to another part of the city. He had found in the desk a bit of paper, with a scrawled address thereon.

It was a certain number in Brooklyn, and inside the hour the detective was across the river.

It did not take him very long to reach the house, which he found darkened and silent, but his ring brought footsteps downstairs and to the door.

As the portal opened Carter caught sight of an old man's face, and he addressed him.

"I desire to see Mr. Holden, your roomer."

"He's sound asleep, sir."

"I must see him all the same. Which room does he occupy?"

The detective pushed forward, with one hand on the old man's arm, and the old fellow seemed to suspect the truth.

"Don't disturb my wife. She's sick upstairs. You shall see Mr. Holden. I hope he isn't a fugitive from justice, sir?"

There was no answer by the detective, for the old man opened a door and motioned Nick across another threshold.

As Carter entered the room a human figure sprang from a bed and stood on the carpet before him.

"How are you?" said the detective.

The reply he got was a snort like a sound from a restive tiger, and George Richmond, brought to bay, threw a swift glance toward the door.

"What's wanting?" he demanded.

"I want you."

"What for?"

"For conspiracy."

The man before Carter seemed to catch his breath.

It was not so bad after all.

In fact, a grim smile appeared at the corners of his mouth and his look softened.

"Who are you?" he next asked.

"Come, you know me, George," said the detective. "I'm not disguised."

"Well, here I am."

The half-dressed man stepped forward, but the moment Carter advanced a step he picked up a chair and with the fury of a maniac threw it above his head.

The old landlord behind the detective uttered a terrified cry and retreated, and as he held the only light there was, the room was wrapped in darkness.

Carter struck a match, and at the same time thrust forward his revolver.

But the match revealed nothing.

George Richmond was gone!

For half a minute Carter stood like a person in a dream, but a sudden cry from the old man aroused him.

"He's crept under the bed, sir," was the cry.

With a light laugh Carter sprang forward and caught hold of the foot he found.

The next moment a bullet whizzed past his head and then he dragged the rascal forth.

Lying on the floor, handcuffed, George Richmond looked up into Carter's face and grinned.

"For conspiracy, eh?" he said. "That's news to me."

"It's better for that than murder," was the answer, and then Carter took his prisoner away.

"Now for the other birds," said the detective, as he turned from the station house.

He proceeded uptown and, late as it was, rang the bell of the Lamont mansion.

For some time no one answered him, and then he heard footsteps inside.

"It's Opal herself," thought Carter, as he waited for the door to open.

Yes, it was the handsome daughter of the dead millionaire, and she maintained her composure as she looked into the detective's face.

"It's a late call, miss," said Carter, as he stepped inside. "But it is a case of necessity. I've found your father."

"Indeed?"

How terribly cool this girl was.

"Yes; he's been found and will be home shortly."

"That's clever of you. I did not know you were looking for him. He went off a little unexpectedly, you see——"

"I understand. He is dead——"

"Father dead?"

It was a real start now, but in a moment Opal regained her composure.

"Miss Lamont, did you ever know a man named Lewis Newell?"

She fell back and seemed to gasp for breath.

"Lewis Newell?" she echoed, trying to become calm again. "I don't know that I ever knew such a man."

"You did not decoy him to a dungeon? You did not coolly let him perish there? I've read his last words on the wall, miss. I know that that is not your only crime!"

"It is false!"

She looked defiant and her eyes flashed.

"There's another, miss," continued Carter.

"You dare not say that again."

"I say it again. There's another crime. It is the greatest one of all."

"What is it, pray?"

"The murder of Mother Flintstone!"

CHAPTER XXXVIII.
JUSTICE'S ROUND-UP.

Opal Lamont seemed to grow into a statue before the detective.

She did not move a muscle, but her face grew white, and the detective thought she would sink to the floor.

But suddenly she started up and calmly invited Carter into the parlor.

The detective accepted and watched her like a hawk, for had not she once faced him with a revolver, and was not this the woman named by "Lewis Newell" on the wall of the dungeon?

Opal Lamont seemed calm now.

She faced the man of many trails and even smiled.

"The murder of Mother Flintstone?" she said, recalling the detective's words in the hall. "You accuse me of that, do you?"

"Yes."

"Let me see your proofs, please."

Carter dived one hand into his bosom and drew forth a little packet, upon which the eyes of Opal Lamont were riveted from the first.

He had never shown this to any one.

No one knew that he found it in an obscure corner of Mother Flintstone's den the night he went thither with Mulberry Billy, the street waif, and the old woman's "chum."

Opal leaned forward and watched the hands of the detective open the packet.

She never took her eyes from the "find," and when the last bit of covering had been taken off she appeared to grow white.

One-half of a ring lay in Carter's hand, and he glanced from it to the immobile face of the millionaire's daughter.

"You found that in the house, I suppose?" asked Opal.

"Yes; in the darkest corner, not far from the spot where you struck the blow."

"Is that all?"

"Not quite."

"You need not go on. Look at me, Mr. Carter. It was for the honor of this house. She was wicked."

"She was your father's sister!"

"She made a bad match. She was disowned, or, rather, she disinherited herself."

"But that was no excuse for the crime."

"She might have paraded the relationship before the world," cried Opal. "She was positively dangerous. She was a perpetual menace. It was dreadful."

"You took it upon yourself to put her out of the way. You went to the house——"

"To silence her tongue!" broke in Opal Lamont. "Murder was not in my mind at first. But she taunted me; she laughed at me when I offered to make her rich. She even threatened to appear in public and boast of the kinship. That was more than I could stand."

"You struck her then?"

"I did. I broke the ring with the blow. I did not miss it till I came home. The other half strangely clung to my finger till I reached this house. I thought I had lost the rest on the street."

"You nearly involved others in that crime."

"How's that?"

"Your brother was for a time suspected of the murder, and then his chum, George Richmond."

"Did it deceive you?"

"For a time. I traced out the ownership of the ring. I did it with the utmost secrecy. But a short time ago I half believed that one of them was the guilty person, but I am undeceived now."

A haughty smile came to the girl's lips.

She made an impatient gesture and then said:

"Let us dismiss these things. We can come back to them, you know. You said a while ago that father was dead."

"He is."

"Where is he?"

"In one of the many houses he owned."

"I thought he would take his life in his madness. He would have given his wealth for the keeping of the secret of the kinship. How did he do it?"

For a moment Carter was silent.

"It was not suicide," said he, looking at Opal. "It was the greater crime—murder!"

She started like one electrified.

"Another murder? I want to see him avenged, even if I have hands that are red! I want you to take the trail of his slayer. You will do this, Mr. Carter? You won't refuse to become the servant of your human quarry?"

"It is no mystery," was the reply. "The murder of your father is not a puzzle!"

"Then you know——"

"I know, for I have a living witness."

Opal was silent; but her deep eyes seemed to pierce the detective through and through.

"I'm calm now. Name him."

At this moment the front door opened and some one came in.

"It is Claude, my brother," said the girl, scarcely above a whisper. "Wait a minute. He may go upstairs."

Carter looked toward the door and seemed to smile.

"Call him in here. His coming will answer the question you have just put."

Opal sprang across the carpet and opened the door, revealing the figure of Claude in the main hall.

"This way, Claude," said she. "A gentleman wants to see you."

It was a lightning glance that passed from the hallway to the man in the parlor.

Claude Lamont knew the detective at once.

He hesitated, but Opal clutched his sleeve and pulled him forward by main force.

"You know this man. It is the trailer," she said.

A dark scowl came to the young man's face.

"I know him!" he almost hissed.

The next instant the daughter turned again to Carter and exclaimed:

"Now, go on. You said you knew who killed father. Name the murderer."

The hand of the detective was raised as his figure straightened, and in a second it covered the young man before him.

"There's the man!" was all he said.

Though he spoke in low tones the words seemed to ring throughout the handsome parlor.

Claude Lamont grew white and Opal fell back.

Suddenly, however, she started forward and paused in front of her speechless brother.

"Is it true?" she cried.

There was no answer.

"You must speak! You must tell the truth. My hands are red and yours seem to be! You have heard this merciless trailer. He says you are a parricide! Is it true? Before Heaven, answer me, Claude Lamont!"

The lips of the young sport moved, but no words issued forth.

He seemed to have been struck with palsy.

"You heard me, murderer!" cried Opal, flinging herself upon her brother. "You must not stand there like a log and say nothing. You shall tell the truth. You did it."

Claude flung her off and she nearly toppled against the mahogany table.

"I did it, and under the circumstances I would do it again!" he exclaimed. "He was coming at me like a wild beast, and I had to fight or perish."

"Swear this!" cried the girl.

Claude raised one hand above his head.

"Where did you find him?"

"On the street."

"But you did not bring him home?"

"I did not. I took him to one of our houses——"

"And killed him there? Murderer!"

That instant, with the fury of a madman, Claude turned upon his sister and covered her white face with his quivering hand.

"Murderer, eh? What are you? Don't you know that the curse of blood has been upon this house for years? The curse of blood and money! Nearly a century ago one of your ancestors murdered his bride, and ever since the stain has been upon the house. It has skipped a few generations, but it is with us now. Richmond and I have kept your red secret. We know who killed Mother Flintstone. Does the detective know?"

"He knows," calmly answered Opal.

"And does he know that the girl called Margie Marne is the grandchild of Mother Flintstone?"

Nick nodded.

"That's all."

Claude Lamont turned and stalked coolly from the room.

At the door he stopped and looked back.

"I'll be on hand when wanted," he said. "It was self-defense. I had to take the old man's life."

Carter and Opal heard him on the stairs, and in a few moments they heard a door shut overhead.

Long before morning a policeman stood guard over the dead millionaire's mansion.

The night passed slowly.

New York was getting ready to awake to the solution of another murder mystery and another crime.

The detective was making the last move in the office of the chief of police, who had listened to the story of his last trail.

George Richmond lay in the station-house cell fast asleep, just as if he had never been concerned in the plot to rob Perry Lamont, the millionaire, with the aid of his scapegrace son.

The morning broke.

Carter went to the Lamont mansion.

Upon parting the night before Opal had pledged her honor that she would greet him when he came again.

He entered the house, speaking first to the guardian at the door, who assured him that all was well, and then he entered the parlor.

He rang the silver call bell on the table, and a servant entered.

"Your mistress?" said he.

"She is upstairs."

Something in the servant's tones attracted the detective, and he bounded up the steps.

Into the girl's boudoir he burst, to stop just beyond the threshold.

One glance was enough—one look at the form lying on the couch satisfied the detective, and he did not remove the black-handled dagger from the blood-flecked bosom.

Claude was found fast asleep and was taken away, but the murderess was left alone.

The trail was ended.

Opal, the murderer of Mother Flintstone, was past reach of judge or jury, and the court acquitted Claude, for Bristol Clara, the only living witness, had to testify in his favor.

George Richmond was tried for conspiracy, and, as the law had long wanted to get another hold on him, he was sent "up the river" for a long term, which proved his last, for he died in Sing Sing.

The outcome of the detective's trail was a startling surprise to Gothamites and became the talk of the town.

Margie Marne received a goodly share of the Lamont wealth, and afterward married, while Mulberry Billy, who played no insignificant part in the Mother Flintstone affair, was placed beyond want by Margie, who had formed an attachment for the boy.

It afterward turned out that Lewis Newell was a man who once persecuted Opal with his attentions, and the girl, with the coolness of a Borgia, decoyed him to his doom and thus began her career of crime.

Carter was highly complimented upon the result of his last trail, but he will never forget his adventure in the dungeon to which he had been decoyed by the daughter of the millionaire, nor the coolness with which she met the terrible charge he brought home to her under her own roof.

THE END.